WHITE OFFERINGS

ANN ROBERTS

Bella
BOOKS
2008

Bella Books, Inc.
P.O. Box 10543
Tallahassee, FL 32302

Printed in the United States of America on acid-free paper
First Edition

Editor: Christi Cassidy
Cover designer: LA Callaghan

ISBN-10: 1-59493-121-6
ISBN-13: 978-1-59493-121-5

Acknowledgments

I'll admit my ignorance about many things, and I'm indebted to those who know more than I—

LC for her knowledge of police work
My buddy Abe for his techno-savvy
Linda Hill and everyone at Bella for their support
Christi Cassidy who makes my writing better each time our paths cross
Amy, who teaches me about myself, love and so much more

This one's for Alex, my son, the future budding writer. Someday you'll be old enough to read your mother's books.

No, not yet.

About the Author

Ann Roberts is a lifelong educator who lives in Arizona with her family. She is the author of *Paid in Full*, *Furthest from the Gate*, *Brilliant* and *Beach Town*. She can be reached at annroberts.net.

Chapter One
Saturday, October 14th
2:13 AM

The sound of pounding feet grew louder and meant one thing—he was closer. She willed herself to move faster, cursing the tight skirt and stiletto pumps that slowed her down. He sloshed through several puddles on the dark street, ones she'd avoided just moments before. She realized he'd already turned the corner and she was in view. A narrow alley lay ahead, illuminated by a naked, yellow bulb that hung over a massive steel delivery door.

She'd wheeled to her right heading toward the alley when her heel settled into an ancient pothole. She gasped and lurched forward. Gravity demanded she fall, ending the chase and her life, but she fought to stay upright, her strong legs and back preventing a collision with the concrete. She increased her speed again, but her ankle screamed in pain. The misstep cost her valuable seconds, and she knew he was gaining on her. Resisting the urge to look back, she pumped her arms harder and entered the black mouth of the alley. Darkness lay ahead and there was no way out. At any point she could careen into a brick wall or fence, but the alternative was worse.

Her ankle throbbed and her feet slowed. He was right behind her, his heavy breathing audible. If she could reach the end of the alley, a sliver of hope existed. She lengthened her stride and felt a hand graze her shoulder. She cried out and lunged forward. He reached for her again, this time grabbing some strands of hair, but she kept going. And then the pavement beneath her disappeared.

Jane's eyes flew open and she gasped, a spasm of terror shooting through her body. The one-night stand sleeping next to her didn't awaken. She glanced at the window and the slash of moonlight illuminating the bedroom. She sat up slowly, her head lolling between her knees. She knew before she looked at the nightstand that the digital display on her clock would show it was somewhere around two. Sure enough, it was 2:13. When her heart rate returned to normal, she rose from the bed, realizing this was the third nightmare in less than a week. She moved toward the window, conscious she was naked but comforted by the bright full moon.

She saw it instantly, haloed by the nearby streetlight. A white orchid lay on her front walk.

Chapter Two

Saturday, October 14th

7:55 AM

A shrill ring ripped Ari from a deep sleep. She dislodged herself from Molly's strong arms and reached for her cell phone. "Ari Adams."

"God, Ari, I'm sorry to call this early, but I waited as long as I could. I've been up since two this morning, so I figured if I wake up my best friend at eight on a Saturday, after sitting in my condo for six terrifying hours already, then I'm still being rather considerate, don't you think?"

She rubbed her eyes, still half asleep. "Sweetie, slow down. I can't understand everything you're saying."

"I got another orchid during the night. Somebody left it on my front walk, and now I'm totally freaking out."

"Oh, no. Okay, honey. It's okay."

Molly sat up, her face full of concern.

3

She covered the mouthpiece and whispered, "Jane got another orchid."

Molly shook her head and fell back against the pillow. "She needs to hire a PI."

She stroked Molly's blond curls as Jane continued to rant. While she loved Jane dearly, it was difficult to know whether a true emergency existed or if her melodramatic nature was responsible for the quake in her voice. Jane continued to barrel through her description while Molly kissed each of Ari's fingertips, and she struggled to focus on the conversation. She knew it would only be a matter of seconds before Molly began sucking on each one, an act of foreplay she couldn't resist.

"Ari, what should I do?" Jane moaned.

Molly's lips closed around her middle finger, and Ari swallowed a sigh. "Jane, why don't we meet at my office at ten? I'm not having an open house today, but I have to go in to do some paperwork. We can have some coffee and talk, okay?" She hoped she didn't sound too rushed.

"Wait a minute," Jane said suspiciously. "Are you with Molly? You are, aren't you? You guys are doing it. Holy shit, Ari! I'm trying to talk to you about my potential murder, and you're getting it on with your girlfriend."

She took a deep breath. "Jane, there's nothing I can do right now. Give me a couple hours and I'll help you figure this out. I promise. If it takes all day, we'll work on it, okay?" She knew the prospect of spending a whole day together while talking about herself would definitely appeal to Jane.

Jane sighed. "Fine. I just hope that I'm not kidnapped or tortured between now and then. You'll feel really bad if my maimed and mutilated body goes undiscovered for weeks."

"No, I'd find it before then. I'll see you in a few." Before Jane could respond, she flipped her phone shut and tossed it on the nightstand. She retreated back into Molly's pleasurable embrace, savoring the gentle kisses Molly planted on her collarbone.

"I take it Jane is upset."

"Yes, this is the fourth orchid that someone has left. I'm beginning to get a little worried about this."

Molly's expression sobered, and much to Ari's dismay, she sat up on her elbow. "Tell me again, when did this start?"

"About two weeks ago. She found the first one in her cubicle at work. She didn't think anything of it. She thought maybe a grateful client had left it. She'd closed a few deals that week, and she assumed it was from one of them."

"Did she check that out? Make some phone calls?"

Ari shook her head. Molly stared at the far wall, lost in her thoughts. She knew Molly was moving deeper into cop mode, and once Detective Molly Nelson fully crowded her entire persona, she might as well get out of bed and start the day. "Jane hasn't done anything proactive. She just has her suspicions." She snuggled against Molly and kissed her cheek, allowing her hands to roam across her body. "I really don't want to talk about Jane anymore. I'll help her figure it out later."

Molly cupped Ari's face in her hands. "You need to promise me that you won't do anything dangerous."

She bit her lip. She'd nearly been killed a few months before, and while she doubted she would ever face that much danger again, she knew Molly was overly cautious about her life. She stared into Molly's crystal blue eyes. "I'll be careful." It would be the perfect opportunity to share her feelings, but she knew Molly wasn't ready to hear the words.

Molly kissed her and smoothed her hair. "I just . . . well, I worry."

She knew it was the closest Molly would come to voicing her feelings. "I know."

A look of relief crossed Molly's face. "She needs to hire a PI. The police won't do anything because technically no crime has been committed."

"I promise I'll suggest that to her when I see her," she said, quickly dismissing Jane's problems. She would spend the day with Jane, but right now she was in bed with Molly, who also was slated to work a stakeout in a few hours. It was a step toward promotion, and it meant Molly would spend more time on the job. She was not going to waste precious moments of intimacy on other matters. She rolled on top of Molly and made sure the next hour was quality time.

Chapter Three

Saturday, October 14th

9:28 AM

Molly parked the Chevy Caprice along the curb across from the industrial office park. Her partner, Andre Williams, handed her a black coffee and reclined the passenger seat to accommodate his lanky frame. Neither of them spoke; they had exhausted all small talk yesterday afternoon. Today was their third day in a joint stakeout with the FBI, and although other officers had told her that this operation, which had accidentally fallen into her lap, was a key to promotion, the waiting was killing her. She glanced at Andre, who looked more like a Wall Street financier than a cop in his well-pressed, dark gray suit and perfectly knotted tie. She surveyed her own appearance. It was a Saturday and for her that meant business casual—jeans, button-down shirt and a sports blazer. She'd grown accustomed to their fashion differences and she had accepted, for the most part, that he would always look more professional.

She sipped her coffee and gazed through the windshield at the brown metal door that had become the center of their lives for the last few days. The FBI was sure that New York crime lord Vince Carnotti was running his Arizona drug operation through this nondescript industrial office complex that sat just south of Phoenix Sky Harbor International Airport. The Cactus Airpark was a lookalike for the six other facilities that lined Mohave Road. It was the ideal place to go unnoticed since the tenants' hours varied and traffic was inconsistent. A plane could glide through the large double doors that were common to each building, and she knew these establishments were ripe for hiding whatever, or whoever, didn't want to be seen.

The radio squawked and the familiar voice of Connie Rasp, the lead field agent for the detail, warbled through the static. "Nora twenty-six, come in."

Molly grabbed the microphone. "Go ahead."

"Morning. You guys got anything out there?"

"Negative."

Rasp sighed. "Nothing here either, and no sign of your informant. Hang tight."

Molly frowned. "Copy."

"That's not good," Andre said.

She swallowed hard and tried to push aside the worry that crept into her mind. Dudley Moon, known as Itchy on the street, was one of her informants and the reason she and Andre had become involved with the feds. He had been busted ten days ago for fencing stolen goods, and when the arresting officers found a pound of cocaine in the pocket of his army jacket, he refused to talk to anyone but Molly. He had insisted he wasn't running drugs, but he was vague about the details, except that the drugs belonged to the Carnotti family. She convinced him to make a deal, knowing he wasn't the prison type. A small, skinny man who looked like a teenager even though he was almost thirty, he knew he'd be somebody's slave within the first week of incarceration. Self-preservation and a belief that the government could protect him drove Itchy to become a snitch.

Apparently when Special Agent Connie Rasp saw Molly's interview tape, she was impressed and immediately asked Molly and Andre to join her two-year-old investigation of the Carnotti family. Itchy was the first person willing to cross the Carnottis in over a year, and Rasp had told Molly that she needed him to stay alive and testify. Her last witness had conveniently crashed into the guardrail of a bridge in Newark when the brakes of his car went out.

Now Molly worried that Itchy might be in danger. She had asked permission to follow him herself, but Rasp had insisted the fibbies take that responsibility, and Molly and Andre were relegated to watching the brown metal door, the place where Itchy said he would bring Carnotti's associates.

"What time is Ari's birthday party?" Andre asked.

"We're getting there around eight thirty, so you could come at eight." She looked at her partner, whose hand tapped the doorframe to a rhythm he heard in his head. "You know, this party might get a little wild. I mean, it's mostly lesbians."

Andre chuckled. "You think a handsome black man can't handle a room full of gay women? I'll bet you that at least one of your sisters swings both ways, and she and I will leave together, or I'll meet one of your few straight friends who's looking for a man."

"I don't know about that."

Andre turned in his seat and pointed at her. "I will bet you lunch for a week that I hook up with a fine woman at your girlfriend's party. You wanna take that bet?" He held out his hand to shake.

She met his grip and smiled. "I don't mind eating pastrami on rye from Duck and Decanter for a week. You're on."

"And no coaching your friends, either," he added. "Keep it aboveboard."

"No problem." Molly glanced at the door, which remained

closed with no activity around the building. Every parking space was vacant and no one entered or exited through the front gate. In fact, she had not seen a single car pass by the other buildings. *Typical Saturday morning*, she thought. But when she reviewed the past two days, she realized they had seen few vehicles and only two or three people. She assumed that many of the buildings were vacant, as evidenced by the handful of real estate signs that lined the fence. Yet, now she wondered.

"Don't you think it's weird that there's no one here?"

Andre shrugged. "It's Saturday morning. I think this is probably normal."

"Yeah, but this isn't much different from the workweek. There's been hardly any action. We saw a few cars, but this place is *too* quiet." She got out and strolled across the street, Andre following behind.

"Mol, what are you doing?"

"We need to check this out. Did the fibbies think to run the water bills on these buildings?"

"I don't know. They told us to sit in the car and watch the door, which you're *not* doing, by the way."

She ignored his protests and strolled past the huge double doors, stopping in front of the main office. She peered between the partially closed slats of the cheap vertical blinds, expecting to see a reception area with a desk and chairs, but instead she saw an empty room, bits of paper scattered on the floor and the phone wires hanging out of the wall. "Shit. Take a look."

Andre stepped to the glass while her temper flared. They had wasted two days of their lives. He looked up, a puzzled expression on his face. "What's going on?"

She stalked across the asphalt to the next building, in view of the other detail assigned to watch the industrial park. She knew it wouldn't take long before Connie Rasp was calling her. She found another window. The inside was the same—down to the hanging phone wires. She headed toward a third building, where she was sure she'd seen a visitor during the week. She peered through the glass and saw a disaster. The furniture was still there, but an entire filing cabinet had been overturned and files lay strewn all over the floor. She imagined someone had broken in or had left in a hurry.

"This is a setup," she said to Andre. He looked through the window just as her radio squawked.

"N twenty-six! What the hell are you doing?"

"There's nothing here. The whole place is empty. They knew we were coming and they got out." Molly waited for a reply, and when she heard nothing, she knew Connie Rasp was already in her car and barreling over to the airpark.

She and Andre had just returned to their vehicle when Rasp's unmarked Ford pulled up beside them. She was out the passenger's side before the car made a full stop. A well-built, handsome African-American woman who was shorter than Molly by six inches, she stepped into Molly's physical space, her anger palpable.

"What the fuck are you doin', Nelson? Who do you think is running this investigation? Who told you to move your ass out of your car? Was it you?" She pointed her finger at Andre, who shook his head fiercely. "This is what I get for working with locals." She placed her hands on her hips, her lips pursed, and waited for Molly's reply.

"This place is a shell," Molly said quietly. She knew Rasp was furious, and she didn't care if she was thrown off the investigation. It would give her more time to look for Itchy. Her anxiety was over the top, now that she was sure he would never make a meeting at Cactus Airpark. "Go look in the windows."

She pointed at the closest office and watched Rasp cross in front of her. Molly's eyes naturally went to the woman's fine figure, particularly her tight ass, which she displayed effectively in her black dress pants. She sighed and chastised herself. *What are you doing noticing other women? You love Ari and you come unglued when she does the same thing. C'mon, Nelson.*

"Damn it," Rasp said when she returned. She went back to

her car and barked at the other detail in her radio. "All units report back to headquarters."

Andre and Molly watched Rasp's car turn around and leave before climbing inside the Caprice.

"She could have at least said thank you," Andre said.

"I don't want a thank you. I want to know where the hell Itchy is."

Chapter Four
Saturday, October 14th
10:03 AM

When Ari pulled up to Southwest Realty, Jane Frank was already sitting on the porch, her cell phone glued to her ear. Ari could see her long, pink nails gesturing with the conversation, which clearly wasn't pleasant. Her perfectly painted face, coiffed brown hair and designer suit created the consummate image of a professional businesswoman. When she was dressed like a conservative Republican, no stranger would ever suspect that her closet harbored her true self—a wild dyke with enough sex toys to start her own adult store. There were, though, very few lesbians in Phoenix who were strangers to her bedroom.

Women adored Jane and gravitated to her physical beauty and extraordinary charm. Her fiery personality burned high most of the time, feeding primarily on anger or passion. Fear and vulnerability were foreign concepts, and if she ever felt anxious or nervous, she hid those emotions from Ari—until recently, until the appearance of the orchids.

Jane looked up and waved. Her eyes narrowed in protest to the phone conversation, and several times she tried to interrupt, only to close her mouth in futility. Ari smiled, amused. She was sure Jane was talking to Aspen Harper, her least favorite client and Phoenix's new, premier chef. Aspen was intent on debating and arguing every point of the transaction with her. Ari imagined the commission must be quite hefty if Jane agreed to endure Aspen's constant scrutiny and second-guessing, even late at night when she would call, anxious about her first home purchase. They had spent two months searching for the perfect house, one that didn't seem to exist.

Ari unlocked the converted bungalow and Jane followed her through the quiet hallways to her office, prattling away with standard responses and soothing words of encouragement. Ari glanced into the spacious main office as they passed its door, surprised that her boss, Lorraine Gonzalez, had not arrived. Lorraine rarely skipped Saturdays, spending much of her weekends hosting open houses or previewing listings with clients. She had the strongest work ethic Ari had ever seen, and she admired the mother of four who believed that hard work was the key to success and a guarantee that her family would never return to their impoverished roots.

Jane dropped onto the divan, pushed the speakerphone button and set her cell phone on the coffee table. She flipped off her heels and hung her stockinged feet over the arm of the couch, withdrawing a nail buffer from her purse to work on her manicure. She no longer bothered to create responses for Aspen, who, like a car running out of gas, eventually exhausted her statements and questions.

"Jane, are you listening to me?"

"Of course, darling. I understand your position entirely. Now why don't you let me worry about your new abode and you focus on those soufflé recipes you were telling me about. They sound marvelous."

"They're amazing," Aspen agreed. "I'm putting them out as the specials tonight."

Jane smiled at Ari. She knew she'd won this round. "I've got to go. Let me know if you need anything."

"Will I see you later?" Aspen asked, almost in a childlike voice.

Jane closed her eyes and gritted her teeth. "I'm sure I'll catch up with you this afternoon. 'Bye." She disconnected and stared at Ari. "Why are we in this business?"

"To make a ton of money, honey," a voice answered. "At least when the market cooperates."

They looked up to see Lorraine Gonzalez in the doorway. A perky woman in her forties, her beautiful smile masked the hard life she'd known before opening Southwest Realty. She was full of curves, as Jane described her, and the tailored suit she wore accented her buxom bosom. She tapped her fingers on the doorjamb and glanced between the two women. "What are you doing here?"

"I got another orchid," Jane said.

Lorraine shook her head. "That's really creepy. You've probably got a stalker."

"Oh, please don't use that word," Jane whined.

"Whoever it is probably has a horrible crush on you and just wants your attention. You are irresistible." Lorraine leaned over and kissed Jane on the head before going back to her own office.

"Why isn't that woman gay?" Jane mused. "You know, I've been told that I *do* have the power to turn straight women gay. Why doesn't she succumb to my charms?"

Ari laughed and joined her on the divan. "Because, honey, Lorraine loves men almost as much as you love women. The only difference between the two of you is that she's much more discreet."

"I'm discreet."

15

"Janey, your name is plastered on bathroom stalls in all of the lesbian bars. Women have written testimonials about your prowess in the bedroom and put them on the Internet. It's not discreet if I can Google you and know about your sex life."

She shrugged, admitting her reputation. "Do you think the orchids are from one of my past conquests?"

"I don't know. It's possible. It would certainly make sense, sweetie. Most women think that going to bed leads to a relationship or a commitment. You've left a trail of women in the dust and some of them have been pretty angry. How many times have you changed your phone number?"

"I'm always honest with them. I've never promised any woman anything. And to answer your question, only three times in the last year. I don't think that's big deal. Most of the women I see understand our relationship, or rather the fact that the word is not in my vocabulary."

"That's true but, honey, all it takes is one."

Jane looked out the window, and Ari knew she was filing through the past few months of lovers. Ari could name at least six different women Jane had bedded recently, and she was sure there were many more. Jane loved women, met them frequently and didn't hesitate to fornicate anywhere.

"I just don't think it's a woman," she mused. "It's too awful to think a woman would stalk another woman like that. In my nightmares it's always a man."

"How do you know?"

"His feet. I hear his shoes against the pavement and they aren't stilettos. It sounds like I'm being chased by an elephant."

"The question is what you should do about it. Molly told me this morning that there's nothing the police can do since no crime has been committed. I'll bring it up with her again if you really want me to, but she's got a lot on her mind with this new assignment. It might get her a promotion."

"And I can tell you're absolutely thrilled by the possibility." She nudged her shoulder. "C'mon, best friend. What's going on

16

between the two of you? I know there's something you're not telling me."

"It's just . . . it's just . . ." Ari sighed. "I can't explain. We've hit some sort of wall, and I don't know what will happen next."

Jane wrapped her arms around Ari and kissed her on the cheek. "It'll all work out, honey. You both just need to suck it up, say that little L word, you know the one that I can't bring myself to think about, and then you'll live happily ever after."

Ari snorted and rolled her eyes. "I don't picture that happening anytime soon."

"The sooner the better, sweetie." Jane looked around the room. "How do you do this?"

"Do what?"

"Keep your office this neat?"

Ari scanned her desk and credenza, which were uncluttered and free of random sticky notes or phone messages. Her folders were organized, alphabetically, of course, and her to-do list was displayed prominently next to her phone. She could only shrug, knowing Jane would never understand. They sometimes joked that one of Jane's ex-lovers was buried underneath the piles of paper that were stacked around her office. She was fastidious about her manners and appearance, but that vanished at the entrance to her workspace.

Jane extended her legs and wiggled her free toes. "I'm bored with this topic for right now. We can talk about you for a little while. Let's start with your birthday party at Hideaway, which is still somewhat about me since I'm planning it. I guarantee it will be a night of heavy drinking, general debauchery and extreme merriment."

Ari winced at the description. "Please don't forget that there are many straight people coming—granted, they are liberal straight people, but you do tend to blur the lines of decency. Sometimes *I'm* offended."

She patted Ari's knee and laughed. "Don't you worry, honey. Lynne and Brian are helping me plan the party, and they're keeping me on the appropriate side of decency, as you put it."

"And you know my father may come, right? I don't think Hideaway would be the best place for a reunion after nearly four years." She tried to imagine Jack Adams at their favorite bar, witnessing a sea of lesbians in various states of dress, freely displaying their affection for one another.

Jane waved off her concern. "So if he decides to come, we'll go to dinner and then dump him at Sol's before we hit the bar." Sol Gardener was the Phoenix Chief of Police, Jack's best friend and Ari's godfather.

"Hmm. I don't know. I think I'll ask him not to come. It just would be too difficult."

Jane sat up and took her hand. "I understand what you're saying, honey, and in this case you might be right, but you've avoided seeing your father for the last six months. I personally think it's great that he's trying to mend the fences from the past. Does he even know about Molly?"

"No, we've talked on the phone about general stuff and work. He hasn't asked me about my love life and I haven't volunteered."

"He'll find out eventually, sweetie. Molly's too big to hide."

Ari gripped Jane's shoulders. "Promise me that you'll exercise some control regarding this party."

Her eyes narrowed. "Define *control*?"

"Uh, well, that would mean no strippers, no sex toys—"

"Wait! No sex toys? But sex is okay, right?"

"Jane!"

"Hey, I'm just looking for parameters." She chuckled. "Honey, you don't need to worry." She clapped her hands once and sat up on the couch. "Now, back to me. What should I do about this flower business?"

Ari rose and grabbed a notepad from her desk. "Tell me the history again."

"This makes number four in the past month. The first one was left on my desk at the office, the second one was on top of my car outside Hideaway, the third one appeared on the bench in front of my gym locker, and now this one."

"It seems like each one gets a little more personal."

"Damn right. Whoever it is knows where I live, where I work and how I spend my time. I'm totally creeped out."

She tapped her pencil on the notepad. "You said four in the last month. Is that about one a week?"

Jane narrowed her eyes. "Well, that's about right, but the last two were only four days apart."

"Hmm. Well, that could be significant. She *or* he may be losing patience. Can you think of any women you've crushed lately?"

Jane scowled. "Don't say that. You make me sound like a monster. I just like a good time." She looked up at Ari, who stared without comment. She wasn't going to argue with Jane about her reputation with Phoenix's lesbian population. "And no, I have not had a screaming match with any woman in the past month, nor have I needed to duck because a date was throwing a shoe at me. The fall season has clearly been about meeting enlightened women." She held up her chin with an air of dignity.

Ari sighed and sat down on the couch. "Well, then maybe it's somebody who's old-fashioned and is trying to court you."

Jane smirked and shook her head. "I doubt it."

"Maybe you should do what Molly suggested and hire a private investigator, someone who could check out the orchids? See if there's some way to tell where they're grown."

Jane held up her hands. "Why do I need a PI? You've got it all figured out. We could do it together."

"I don't know, Jane. Molly made me promise that I would never again involve myself in anything dangerous. Not after last time."

Jane was silent but her gaze went to Ari's shoulder, the place where Ari had been shot. "I'm just talking about the orchid part," she said. "The simple legwork. No chasing criminals. That'll give me time to look for a real PI. What do you say? Please? I'm really desperate here."

She hated it when Jane whined. She rarely put on a pathetic face, but when she did, it was priceless. She sighed. "Hand me the phone book, and let's look up florists."

Chapter Five
Saturday, October 14th
1:40 PM

The morning had really been about spending time with Jane. They had stopped at three floral shops with detours for her personal needs and her bottomless stomach. Jane seemed to relish their time together. It was like the old days when they both were single. Since she and Molly had become a couple, Jane was relegated to the outer circle of her life, and while she never uttered a complaint, Ari knew she felt a distance growing between them. So she was happy to spend the beautiful day cruising through Phoenix in Jane's convertible Porsche Boxster while everyone stared or honked at the sleek machine.

By afternoon two facts were clear to Ari: Jane was highly connected, and the orchid-sender could be any female in the metropolitan Phoenix area. Despite Jane's belief that someone wanted to harm her, Ari wasn't sure the orchids were meant to be sinister. Jane had brought the last one along to show florists. Ari studied the delicate petals and the beautiful design. It was truly elegant, and as she held the slender stalk in her hand, she thought of Molly, imagining her lover naked on her bed while she stroked her tanned skin with the silky white flower. She quickly set the orchid back in her lap before her thoughts went wild. She couldn't fathom how something so gorgeous could ever carry a dark purpose.

"Lunchtime," Jane announced as she whipped the Porsche into a parking spot at the front door of McGurkee's, their favorite sandwich shop. "You go grab a table and I'll get our usual."

The eatery was crowded, and Ari found the last open booth in a corner by a picture window. She gazed at the buildings across the street and reviewed the morning's activities. They had accomplished little due to their intermittent detours. After stopping at Jane's to retrieve the last orchid, they'd gone to AJ's Fine Foods because Jane couldn't live without her morning double mocha latté. Ari was astonished when Jane greeted the coffee barista with a kiss on the mouth. When they went to pay, she embraced the cashier and turned to Ari. "Lina, this is my best friend in the whole world, Ari Adams."

Lina took her extended hand and brought it to her lips. "Ari, it is a pleasure. Jane has such good taste in friends." The look in her eyes left Ari with a clear message of opportunity. She withdrew her hand and noticed the amused expression on Jane's face.

Their first florist stop proved a dead end, since the only person working was a high school student. The thin young man dressed in gothic attire knew nothing about orchids except that his shop didn't carry them very often, but he thought Jane's flower was quite beautiful. Next they had zipped into the dry cleaners to claim Jane's suits, which also netted her a dinner date with the carhop.

At the second flower shop they learned more about the orchid. The owner, a pudgy older man with white hair, pulled out a thick book on flowers and found the section on orchids.

His gaze shifted from the orchid Jane held in her hand to the array of pictures on the page. When he found what he wanted, his stubby finger smacked the book.

"That's it," he said. "The *Angraecum elephantinum*, also known as the *Gigantic Angraecum*. It's very difficult to grow and must be nurtured carefully."

"Do you sell it?" Ari asked.

The florist shook his head. "No, certainly not something that rare. You wouldn't have much of a market for it. Whoever grew that flower did so out of love, not profit."

"I'd say you have an admirer," Ari told Jane as they left.

"An admirer? What kind of admirer tries to scare the crap out of their intended conquest?"

"Jane, the person may not know he or she is affecting you this way. You heard what the man said. Someone grew it out of love."

"Love of *flowers*, not love for *me*. If I find out who's doing this, I'm going to press charges."

Ari chuckled. So far the entire situation seemed rather benign, and she was rather sure Jane was being overly dramatic. The third stop confirmed that Jane did possess a *Gigantic Angraecum*, but the salesperson did not carry them and had received no inquiries that she could remember.

Ari looked over at the sandwich line to observe Jane shooting a straw wrapper at the drink girl, who giggled. Jane, the naked straw still dangling between her lips, waved it up and down. The girl laughed nervously, clearly embarrassed. Ari shook her head. Jane never knew when to quit. Her phone chimed from the recesses of her purse and she grabbed it before it went to voice mail. She smiled when she saw Molly's name on the caller ID.

"Hey, baby," Ari whispered.

"Hi. How's it going with Jane?"

She could hear concern and fatigue in Molly's voice. No doubt her own investigation was draining her energy, and the idea of Ari chasing a stalker with Jane probably heightened her anxiety.

She knew Molly loved her, even if she wasn't ready to say it. "We're just having fun driving around." She hoped she sounded casual. "Most of the day has been about lattés, dry cleaning and food. We're at McGurkee's right now."

Molly laughed heartily. "Jane and her stomach."

"Exactly. You have nothing to worry about."

"Good. I've got enough going on. The stakeout was a total bust, and now we're regrouping. Anyway, I just wanted to call because you may need to go out to my folks' by yourself and I'll get out there as soon as I can, okay?"

Of course it was okay. Every time Molly asked Ari to spend time with her family, she always made it sound like Ari was shouldered with an unwanted burden. The fact was that she loved Molly's family, particularly Brian and Lynne. The four of them frequently double-dated and spent Saturday nights together making dinner and going to jazz clubs. Tonight they were headed out to Molly's parents' house for Brian's birthday.

"Don't worry about it, babe. I'll pick up the wine and take the gift. Brian is going to love that gearshift knob you found for him." Brian was restoring an old Aston-Martin in his spare time, and Molly had combed the Internet for the parts he wanted. "Do you have any idea how late you'll be?"

Molly sighed heavily. "Uh, probably around eight. Eat without me, but I'll try to make the birthday cake, okay?"

Jane appeared with the food and mouthed Molly's name. Ari nodded in response. "Okay. Take care. 'Bye." She slipped the phone into her purse and frowned. "She's working so hard right now."

Jane grabbed the catsup and filled a small bowl that sat on her tray, preparing to eat her fries. Ari was accustomed to Jane's quirky eating rituals. She rarely ate food with her hands, and her table manners surpassed anything recommended by Emily Post. Only after she had cut a fry in fourths, speared a piece of it with her fork and dipped it into the catsup did she finally bring the morsel to her lips. By then Ari had devoured a third of her entire meal.

"It's because she's trying to get a promotion, right?" Jane asked after she had chewed the fry at least ten times.

"Well, she doesn't have a clear plan, but it's really stressful right now. She was calling to tell me that she'll be late to Brian's birthday party, and I know she's disappointed. Brian is her favorite person in the world."

"No, you are her favorite person in the *world*. He's just her favorite brother. Now, speaking of birthday parties, I think I need a little more clarification. How will Brian and Lynne react if your birthday cake is in the shape of a woman's chest?"

She nearly dropped her sandwich. "Did you get me a boob cake?"

Jane finished chewing thoroughly before she replied. "I have not ordered the cake yet, but I have to do it today. I knew you wouldn't go for a vagina-shaped cake, so I was thinking of breasts."

"What about a rectangular sheet cake? You know, like everyone else has?"

Only after Jane had dabbed the corners of her mouth did she answer. "You are not everyone. You are my best friend, and we are going to make this an incredibly memorable party." She waved her hand, dismissing the subject. "Don't worry. I'll think of something."

Ari was still trying to imagine how a baker could create a vagina-shaped cake as they left the sandwich joint to continue their quest for orchid information. She surmised that if the sender had not purchased the flower from a shop, he or she was growing them in a private greenhouse or buying them off the Internet, if that was possible. In either case, she doubted they would ever find the admirer.

"I need to connect with Teri," Jane said.

She headed east toward the Biltmore area into a small pocket of spacious old ranch houses, many of which sat on huge lots. A rusty banana-yellow Dodge pickup truck was parked in front of a house that seemed out of place for the neighborhood. A modernistic structure full of angles, it was clearly ahead of its time, and it reminded Ari of Frank Lloyd Wright's architectural style.

Jane pulled up behind the truck and sprang out of the Porsche. "I'll be back in a sec."

Ari sighed and turned up the radio. A flash of movement caught her eye and she watched a jackrabbit scurry under a bush. She smiled at the thought of a wild creature still able to survive in the middle of a huge metropolitan area. Not more than fifty years ago most of the valley had been a desert, but now urban sprawl threatened to destroy the eco-balance, and as a real estate agent, she felt slightly guilty.

Five minutes later Jane hurried back to the Porsche with the woman Ari assumed was Teri following behind. While Jane moved swiftly, Teri sauntered, unwilling to hurry, her stride demanding that Jane slow down to match her pace. A true butch, Teri wore a blue tank top with her overalls, revealing a defined upper body that Ari would never attain. Her dark hair was slicked back and wet, as if she'd just stepped out of a shower. Ari stared at the woman, who was all business with Jane, talking about the price of water heaters and the time it would take to install. She glanced briefly at Ari, and Ari was surprised to find a shiver running down her back. She looked away, feeling the heat on her cheeks, pretending to be fascinated by Jane's glove compartment.

At an appropriate pause in the conversation, Jane touched her arm. "Ari Adams, this is Teri Wyatt, handy-dyke extraordinaire."

Teri laughed at Jane's nickname and stuck her hand over the passenger door. "Hi, Ari. I've heard a lot about you. I can't wait for your birthday party."

"Oh," Ari said, surprised. She could only imagine how many total strangers Jane had invited.

"Teri's gutting this house and remodeling it for me," Jane said.

Ari nodded, quite familiar with Jane's many investment properties. She constantly searched through the listings and the Open House section of the newspaper. Although most of the real deals had already been flipped by people like Jane, once in a while a bargain came along. Jane had been thrilled to find this one, and Ari was certain her profit, despite the slumping economy, would reach six figures once Teri was done.

"Are you doing most of the work yourself?" Ari asked with genuine interest. She could always use a good handyperson, and Teri was certainly easy on the eyes.

"I'm doing *all* the work."

"Really?" She was impressed. Few people had the talent and knowledge to run the electrical systems, install the plumbing and hang the Sheetrock.

Jane threw her arm around Teri and patted her shoulder. "Teri's my main lady. If I need anything, I go to her."

Teri smiled humbly at the compliment and checked her watch. "Well, I gotta hurry to Home Depot and pick up my order if I want to get everything done. Ari, it was a pleasure to meet you, and I'll see you tomorrow, Jane."

They watched Teri climb into her truck. She threw them a quick wave before she drove off.

Jane said, "So you think Teri's hot, don't you?"

"She seems nice."

Jane laughed and slid into the Porsche. "Good try, girlfriend. I saw you staring just now. You couldn't take your eyes off her, watching her cute little ass hop into that big king cab."

"I wasn't staring."

"Sure." Jane started the convertible and turned to her. "Look, honey, there's nothing to be ashamed of. You're in a relationship but you're not dead. You can look, and with Teri, there's plenty to look *at*."

"I take it you know from experience."

Jane shrugged. "Not really. Teri's more of a loner. We went out for drinks, and I invited her back to my place. She declined."

27

"She turned you down?"

Jane flicked a lint ball from her jacket and checked her lips in the rearview mirror. "It happens. Besides, she is totally not my type." She crumpled her nose in distaste. "Way too butch."

"I thought every woman was your type."

"Not *every* woman. But I do believe that there is no greater beauty than the female body. And you were certainly checking out her body."

"Jane!"

"Don't worry, honey. I won't kid you about it in front of Molly. I know she's very insecure."

Ari made no comment and they headed to their next stop, a prestigious flower shop in Scottsdale. When they had searched the phone book, Jane had recognized the name, claiming to know the owner. The shop sat on a desirable corner, and the parking lot was nearly full. The automatic doors whooshed open and their noses were instantly assaulted by competing scents. Ari glanced at the various displays around the room, all of which were beautiful and tastefully created.

"How do you know this person?" she asked as they approached the marble counter.

"Oh, you know."

She rolled her eyes. Another one of Jane's sexual conquests, but the entire day had been filled with Jane's bed partners.

A young man in a pink polo crossed the room to meet them. His hips swayed back and forth rhythmically, and even without the pink shirt, she would have known he was family. He flashed two rows of perfectly bleached teeth and asked, "May I help you?"

"I'm looking for . . ."

She realized Jane couldn't remember the name of this particular one-night stand.

"Clarisse?" the young man offered. "Or Isabel?"

Jane clapped her hands together. "Yes, Izzie. Is she around?"

The young man nodded and quickly sashayed into the back.

Ari wandered over to the far wall, which was covered in pictures of orchids. Jane joined her and pointed at the one in the center, the type of orchid that had appeared four times in her life during the past month.

"Jane?" a voice said from behind them.

Ari turned to see a tall, graceful woman approach. She was striking, but what Ari noticed was her sumptuous lips. There were no other words to describe them because they were absolutely perfect, and it seemed to Ari that her other facial features existed to frame her lips. She was dressed in a finely tailored gray suit that molded precisely to her lean body and small waist. Ari was certain the Scottsdale clientele was impressed by her memorable presence, and the woman was certainly Jane's type.

"Izzie!" They hugged as if they were old friends reuniting after a long absence. When Jane pulled away from the embrace, Ari noticed Isabel remained quite close to her.

"What's going on, darling?" Isabel asked. "I thought you would have called me, but I am glad to have a visit instead. How long has it been? Two months?" She attempted to sound playful, but a sharp edge to her tone conveyed her hurt feelings.

"I'm sorry, Izzie. I've been so busy. I hope you understand. I told you how I am with dating, and we did have an incredible time, didn't we?"

Isabel said nothing in response, clearly understanding the meaning of Jane's hollow explanation. Ari doubted if she even remembered Isabel's visit to her bedroom, and Ari suspected it was her carefree attitude about sex that had made her the stalker's target. It was amazing she had not been tarred and feathered by all of the regulars at Hideaway. What Jane couldn't understand was intimacy and commitment and, more importantly, the normal female urge for both. Ari had made endless attempts to explain the female mind to her. Jane, though, was more like a man and loved her sexuality openly. She grimaced every time Ari made the comparison, and it was rather ironic that someone so femme could behave so butch, but Jane did not equate sex with a relationship. The fact that she dated femmes almost exclusively added to the problem, in Ari's opinion. What Jane needed was a good butch.

Isabel considered Jane's apology and quickly forgave her transgression, paving the way for the reason for their visit. "How can I help you?" she asked, her perfect lips forming a professional smile.

"Well, this is my friend Ari."

Isabel turned and gave a slight bow in her direction. "It is a pleasure to meet you, Ari. I'm Isabel Collins."

"Izzie, could you tell us about an orchid?"

"Which one interests you?"

"This one," Ari said, gesturing to the middle flower on the wall, whose slender white petals burst from the center, like long fingers extended in greeting.

Isabel nodded her approval. "That's my favorite. The *Gigantic Angraecum*. It's extremely rare. Usually it grows in Madagascar, but if it can be grown here, it will only bloom with one or two flowers. It is most fragrant at night."

"Have you been able to grow it?" Ari asked.

Isabel smiled in pride. "Of course. My greenhouses are extensive, and my attention to my flowers is unparalleled." Isabel paused and her face colored. "But as you can see, Ari, my modesty could use some refinement."

"Is it expensive?"

"Oh, yes. The more exotic a bloom, the greater the price."

"Are there other shops that sell this flower?" Jane asked.

Isabel's eyes narrowed. "Very few, I would imagine. I can only think of two or three in the metro area."

"Is this the kind of flower you could order online or have shipped from somewhere else?"

Isabel frowned. "Certainly not," she said with disgust. "At least *I* would never try to ship such an exotic flower in PB size. It would be very difficult to keep it alive."

"What's PB?"

"Previously bloomed. It's much easier to ship seedlings or nearly blooming flowers, but this flower wouldn't travel well. It is much better to ship flowers when they are in low spike, or just getting started with their buds. It's much less likely they'll be damaged."

Ari suspected as much. She'd surfed the Internet for a few minutes before they'd left her office, and it became apparent that FTD and its counterparts didn't carry the *Gigantic Angraecum*. "How many have you grown?" Ari pressed.

"Some."

Ari noticed that Isabel's gaze drifted to another part of the store. She wasn't sure if it was because there were serious clients needing assistance or if Isabel was trying to hide a lie.

"So I don't suppose most people could afford this flower," Jane joked. Ari saw where she was going with the comment, but Isabel just laughed and continued to look away, her interest in the conversation quickly dwindling.

"Could you give us the names of those other florists, Izzie?"

"Of course." She wrote down the names and held the slip of paper out to Jane. "Have dinner with me tomorrow night." Isabel's tone was unmistakable. She would trade information for another night in Jane's bed.

Without hesitation, Jane plucked the paper from Isabel's fingers, a wide grin on her face. Ari knew she appreciated someone who could drive a bargain.

"That would be wonderful, darling," she said, and Ari thought she was genuinely pleased.

Isabel kissed her on the cheek. "I'll pick you up at seven." She waved good-bye and headed toward her other customers.

"Well, another night with Izzie won't be so bad," Jane said. They climbed into the Porsche and she started the engine.

Ari shook her head, unable to fathom Jane's sexual ethics. "There's something about her that's off."

"What are you talking about? Izzie is amazing. She's really smart. She's got a Ph.D. or something in horticulture and she's

31

totally hot."

"In other words, she's brilliant, knows a lot about flowers and doesn't mind blackmailing you for sex." Jane's jaw dropped and she continued. "She just seems possessive and quite interested in getting her own way."

"I still don't think she sent me those flowers. I'm sure it was a man."

"I'm not," Ari disagreed. "In fact, after a day with you, I'd almost bet a woman is sending you those flowers."

Jane shrugged and steered the Porsche into the closest Starbucks for a shaken black iced tea. They stopped by one of the three flower shops Izzie listed, but the salesclerk hadn't sold any elephant orchids, as Jane now insisted on calling them, in over four months. The day was practically over and Ari demanded that they quit.

As Jane drove back to Ari's office, talking with Aspen Harper on her cell phone headset, Ari thought of Izzie. She reminded her of a spider—cunning, exquisite and dangerous. Ari would never have dated a woman like her. Then it hit her. Never once during their visit had Isabel asked Jane to explain why she wanted to know about orchids.

Chapter Six

Saturday, October 14th
3:18 PM

Molly sank into her desk chair and massaged her temples. They had spent two hours at FBI headquarters analyzing the owners and tenants of Cactus Airpark. A breakdown in communication had occurred and no one had informed Connie Rasp that almost all of the buildings were owned by the same corporation, Johnson Enterprises, a shell company with many arms. One of those was Rondo Dynamics, owned by John Rondo, a cousin of Vince Carnotti. Molly almost laughed when she thought of the confrontation between Rasp and the low-level researcher who had forgotten to e-mail the vital information to her. By the time Rasp finished screaming at him, he walked away without a rear end, having it thoroughly chewed off by her.

Molly located the Tums in her desk drawer and popped four into her mouth to quell her sour stomach. She craved a Scotch but reached for a water bottle instead. Ari had insisted she improve her diet and was now purchasing expensive spring water for her to keep at work. She chugged the contents and searched her hard drive for notes on Itchy. Rasp had instructed her and Andre to find him, and Molly perused some of her notes for the most recent address. She heard footsteps and looked to her doorway, thinking it was Andre.

"I found it," she said.

"What the hell happened, Nelson?"

Standing there with his hands on his hips was Captain David Ruskin, her boss and a man she detested for many reasons. Over the last three years she had learned to hold her temper and answer his questions succinctly. He tended to leave quickly if she refused to let him bait her. "The fibbies screwed up. The meeting place was abandoned, and now Rasp has Andre and me looking for the informant."

"So what are you doing here? Why aren't you out in the field?"

"We had to come back for the address. I don't have it committed to memory." She couldn't stop herself from taking a dig at him. It had been years since he had engaged in any fieldwork. He loved sitting in his office and barking at people. He especially hated her, partly because of his homophobia and mainly because she was with Ari, a woman he desired and couldn't have.

He snorted. "Well, you need to get moving. You're not gonna find the guy sitting on your ass."

"Captain Ruskin, that was uncalled for." Rasp appeared in the doorway next to him, and he seemed to shrink. "If it wasn't for Detective Nelson, we *all* would still be sitting on our asses watching an empty building. You need to congratulate her, not chastise her."

His face turned beet red, and from her desk, Molly could see his jaw set.

Rasp waited and stared him down until he walked away. She watched him go and then came inside and shut the door. When she turned to Molly, she grinned. "How do you work for him?"

"Not well. Hey, thanks. I think you just made my day. What are you doing here?"

Rasp slid into a chair and crossed her legs. Molly noticed she had reapplied her lipstick and pulled her hair back with a clip. She looked sexy, and Molly felt warm all over. She paused before she said, "Unfortunately, I just did it. I came here to personally tell your captain about your effort today, but I guess you won't be getting any pats on the back."

Molly shook her head and stared at her nails. "Not from him. We just tolerate each other." She glanced at Rasp, who cocked her head and folded her arms over her large chest. There was something different about her. She was relaxed, less professional.

"Why does he hate you?"

"Because I'm gay, and because my girlfriend wouldn't go to bed with him, and because her father, a former cop, made his life hell when he was a rookie."

Rasp smiled slightly. "Sounds like a lot of history, and it sounds like he's an ass." She immediately shook her head. "I'm sorry. That was terribly unprofessional of me. So how does your girlfriend know Ruskin? Is she a cop?"

"She was for a brief time. She sells real estate now."

"Ah," Rasp replied. "Couldn't hack it?"

"Didn't want to."

Rasp held up a hand. "Hey, I didn't mean to disrespect your woman."

Molly leaned back in her chair and took a breath. "It's okay. I'm just worried about my informant. What if something's happened to him?"

Rasp folded her hands in her lap and looked away. "We'll just have to see," she said, and Molly realized Rasp thought he was already dead. She stood and faced her. "Well, good job today, detective, and good luck finding your guy." She left, Molly's gaze following her until the door closed softly.

• • •

The odor of the Liberty Apartments was a mixture of rotting drywall, sweat and sewage. Molly had no idea how anyone could tolerate the stench, but Itchy lived a step away from homelessness most months, and she imagined he didn't care as long as he had a room to himself. She'd never been to his place, but he'd told her about it during one of their meetings at the Chase Field parking garage. She was very worried now that Itchy, who was relatively harmless on the criminal food chain, had been declared a missing person.

The rooming house sat on Madison Street, two blocks from the jail. *This is a flophouse*, she thought as she and Andre ascended the rickety steps. She didn't hold the banister for fear of splinters from the cracked and decayed wood, and she watched the floor, concerned that a roach or a rat would scurry across her loafer at any moment. The peeling wallpaper and the single lightbulb illuminating the stairwell reminded her of a haunted house at Halloween. They found Itchy's room—the door slightly ajar. Andre looked at her, and they both drew their weapons. No one was inside the sparse living quarters. His dresser drawers were open, and it was clear that the place had been searched, but she imagined the other residents were to blame.

"It looks like some folks borrowed his stuff," Andre said. He held up two pieces of a flashlight, the batteries missing, thus confirming her theory.

"We need to go through everything carefully," she said, pulling on a pair of latex gloves. "There might be a clue to his whereabouts and something that links him to Carnotti."

They dug through separate corners, checking the pockets of his clothes and rummaging through the shoeboxes full of his possessions. Itchy compartmentalized his belongings so they would fit into a shopping cart in a minute should he ever become mobile. She found several photos of a beautiful woman sitting on a sofa with a small boy whose face reminded her of Itchy. She guessed the lady must be his mother.

"Molly, check this out," Andre called from the closet.

He held up a backpack, the one Itchy always carried with him. She couldn't imagine where he would be without it. Andre dumped all of the items out and they picked over them—a few sticks of gum, a can of Coke, a pencil, his Will Work for Food sign, seven dollars, his driver's license and a bus pass for a woman named LaDonna Jones.

"Nothing here," he said.

Molly looked around the room, certain that they were missing something. No doubt Itchy's disappearance was tied to what he knew and who he knew, but he was shrewd. She remembered the first time she ever traded for information. He had fingered a drug dealer in return for a future favor from her, a marker he could claim later. Later was six months, when he called her one afternoon and needed fifty bucks to make his weekly rent. He was the only street person she had ever known who possessed foresight and an ability to plan. Now, as she stood in his run-down room, she was certain there was a clue that he was keeping in reserve. Her gaze returned to the filthy backpack. It was what he valued the most. She unzipped the bag and pulled both sides apart like an unfolded sandwich, carefully searching the small inner pockets. She found nothing, and she was about to give up when she noticed a small zipper in one of the straps. She unzipped the secret compartment, and withdrew a slip of paper with four numbers written in pencil—6815.

"What is that? It's too short for a phone number," Andre said.

"I don't know. Maybe it's a locker." She studied the scrap, clearly higher quality, perhaps linen, but it was worn and had been in the backpack for a while. Shaped like a triangle, two sides formed a corner while the longer one was jagged, as if it was torn from a piece of paper. She turned it over and found the words *Here to Help!* written in blue lettering. She held it up for Andre. "I'd say this is an end of one of those memo pads that companies buy with their name and slogan."

"Yeah, and it looks like Itchy tore off a piece to write down this number. We just need to figure out where the pad came from. That'll probably tell us what the numbers mean."

"Maybe. Can you imagine how many companies have *Here to Help* in their slogans? It's a standard line for customer service. And we don't know how long Itchy's had this piece of paper. The company could be out of business or it might be totally unrelated."

Andre grinned. "I'm glad you're approaching this with such optimism." She closed her eyes and shook her head. He squeezed her shoulder and took the slip of paper. "Look, whatever it means, it's important. He kept this in a secret pocket, and that tells me he wasn't interested in seeing it every day. He was saving it to use only if he needed it. This was his insurance policy."

She looked around the room, remembering that the desk clerk had not seen him in nine days, since the day after his meeting with her. "Let's hope it was life insurance."

Chapter Seven

Saturday, October 14th
5:10 PM

Ari took a deep breath as the uncooperative Saturday traffic inched through the Deck Tunnel, every lane packed with Suns fans on their way to the evening preseason game. Purple and orange jerseys and foam fingers appeared in the windows of the cars and SUVs crowding to exit at Seventh Street on their way to US Airways Arena. An enormous Suburban cut her off and crossed two other lanes of irate fans, many of whom honked their horns in protest. Instead of joining in their complaints, she chose to focus on the upcoming evening. Some people dreaded their in-laws, and although she would never call the Nelsons her "relatives" in front of Molly, she thought of them as family, the family she had lost in her youth. She relished any opportunity to celebrate with them, and unlike many families who only gathered for a specific purpose, she delighted in being with them for no particular reason.

She pulled up next to a sedan and glanced at the couple with their two children sitting in the back, laughing and shouting at each other. Decades ago, that could have been her and her brother, Richie. They always argued in the car, the volume of their fights escalating until their mother turned around to scold them. Ari tried to picture her mother's profile as she would lean over her seat with a serious expression on her face. The snapshot was blurred, and she couldn't remember specific details about her mother. From photos she knew they looked almost identical with raven hair and strong features, but she struggled to hear her mother's voice or recall favorite phrases or expressions her mother would use.

The family had suffered for fifteen years, watching cancer claim Lucia Bianchi Adams one cell at a time. When she finally succumbed to the disease four years ago, Ari had walked away from her father at the headstone and never looked back.

Abandoning him left her entirely alone without anyone to call a family. Richie had died as a child, the victim of a shooting at a convenience store. She had tried desperately to fill the void left by his passing, but she never felt she measured up in her father's eyes. When she had told her parents she was gay, she proved to be a disappointment in the worst of ways to her father. Only in the recent months had he reentered her life, due to Sol's prodding.

Her cell phone rang at that moment, and she glanced at the display to see her father's name on the caller ID. *How weird*, she thought. "Hello," she answered coolly. She still was not ready to answer her father's calls with familiarity and kindness.

"Hi, honey . . . It's Dad," the voice quickly added.

"Hi."

An awkward silence passed and she could tell she had flustered her father. They had been apart for so long and their recent conversations had not fully bridged the emotional distance between them.

"I won't keep you. I just wanted to get some ideas for a birthday present. Do you like tools?"

She grimaced and automatically shook her head in disbelief. "No, Dad. I don't need anything more than what I have. I live in a high-rise condo, so if something breaks, I just call maintenance."

"Huh," he grunted. "I just noticed on TV that women like you were very handy, at least the ones on this home repair show I saw on cable."

"And what kind of woman am I, Dad?" She heard him curse under his breath but he didn't respond. The traffic splintered and she was finally able to hit the accelerator. "Dad?"

"Look, Ari, I don't want to fight. I just need some ideas. Give the old guy a break. If I'm going to learn about your *lifestyle*, I'll need help. I admit it, okay?"

She sighed. He was making an effort and she was being a bitch. "Look, I'm sorry. Buying me a gift isn't that hard. I love to cook, so anything for the kitchen is a good bet, and I love bath products, and books, particularly about architecture, so that gives you something to go on, right?"

"Yeah, that makes it easy."

She could hear relief and surprise in his voice. No doubt Jack Adams had thought he either would be wandering into a dark sex shop to purchase a gift for his lesbian daughter or seeking out a handy bull dyke for advice about the latest home-improvement gadgets.

"Well, I won't keep you."

"So are you coming down?" she asked.

"Uh, I don't know. I'm not sure I'm ready, you know?"

"I understand."

"Are you mad?"

"No, it's okay. I need to go. The traffic is getting heavy," she lied. "I'll talk to you soon."

She flipped the phone shut and spent the rest of her drive deciding if she was angry or relieved that her father might miss her thirty-fifth birthday. A respected police sergeant, he had retired

41

to Oregon, and they had not seen each other since her mother's funeral. It was just too hard. Without her, there was no buffer, no one to stop their dysfunctional conversations from devolving into shouting matches. Whatever relationship they could develop now would be totally up to him, and she had already prepared herself for the disappointment she was certain would come.

She wound her way through the Nelsons' subdivision, scanning the driveways for the twin Nelson Plumbing trucks. It was the only way she could identify the house among an entire row of doppelgangers, all of which were painted muted tans, sported enormous oak front doors and were topped by tile roofs. She would never purchase a cookie-cutter home regardless of its reasonable price, but she had sold many of them and understood the attraction. They were new and full of amenities that families needed. She saw the trucks on her right and pulled up to the curb. She had barely started up the walk when the front door burst open and two children ran down the path to greet her.

"Ari!" they both cried.

She stopped, allowing them to wrap their little bodies around her middle. She couldn't return the hug, her arms loaded with wine and gifts. "Hi, guys." She loved five-year-old Chelsey and her three-year-old brother, Kenny, who treated her as if she was another aunt. "Can you help me carry these things in?" Both blond heads nodded, and she handed each one a present to take into the house. The children ran back through the front door and disappeared.

She stepped over the threshold and amazing smells poured out of the kitchen and loud sports commentary squawked from the plasma TV. Molly's father, Don, and his oldest son, Don Jr., watched the Suns' pregame show while Molly's mother, Teddy, floated across the kitchen, stirring, checking and preparing the entire meal. Theodora Nelson was the old-fashioned kind of mother who wouldn't allow anyone in her domain. The only exception was Don Jr.'s wife, Jenna, since Molly would have nothing to do with cooking. When Teddy had tried to teach Molly her culinary secrets, Molly always found convenient excuses to miss her cooking lessons. There was always a softball game or a flying lesson. Consequently, she never learned to make anything beyond grilled cheese.

"Hi, Ari," Teddy called.

Don Jr. waved and Molly's father jumped up and gave her a hug. "I hear my detective daughter is going to be late."

"She is. She's working on a big case."

"Is it dangerous?" Teddy asked, emerging from the kitchen and giving her a quick hug.

"I don't think so. She's with a lot of other detectives and even some people from the FBI. I think this is really their case."

"Hey, stranger," a voice called. Ari turned to see Jenna coming down the hall. She looked as though she had just awoken from a nap. Ari imagined that Jenna, pregnant with her third child, needed more rest.

Ari kissed her on the cheek and squeezed her shoulder. "How's everything going?"

"Doctor says we're fine. We went in for our first ultrasound and the baby looks healthy."

"Do you know if she's a she or a he?" Ari asked excitedly.

"No, and I don't think we'll find out this time. We've got one of each and plenty of baby clothes for either, so we want to enjoy the surprise."

"I don't," Don said. "I want another boy."

"All you ever wanted was boys," Teddy said, moving back into the kitchen toward the amazing aromas.

"Where are Brian and Lynne?" Ari asked Jenna.

"They're on their way. Brian did some moonlighting work for a friend, and he had a major problem. They should be here in a while. Why don't you open that bottle of wine, pour a glass and relax?"

She left the married women to the work and wandered through the house. She stopped as she always did to look at the family photos that lined the hallway wall. She adored the childhood pictures of Molly, and every time she studied the display, she wondered if she would have liked her when she was nine, or fifteen or twenty-three. Would there have been the unbelievable connection that existed between them now? They shared a variety of common interests, including a passion for old movies, fabulous coffee and making love. Many of their evenings included all three, beginning with great sex and ending with the two of them lounging in bed, sipping a great Sumatran blend while they watched an old classic, preferably a Lauren Bacall flick.

She sighed. Even though they had not said the words, she knew she was in love. Every time she saw Molly her stomach fluttered and a smile crossed her face. Their fiery tempers sometimes stalled their feelings, but neither could stay angry for long, and the make-up sex was incredible. She often teased Molly about her loose past, but her days of one-night stands were over. Molly had not ventured into Hideaway since they had become a couple. They were completely committed to each other, but Ari knew that Molly still felt unworthy of her love and insecure about their relationship.

"When will you leave me?" was Molly's repetitious question, followed by a nervous laugh.

Ari always laughed back, but she could see the fear behind her eyes. "You're all I want."

And as quickly as it had come, the doubt was erased momentarily. Bolstering Molly's confidence, though, was continually necessary, an injection that fueled the romance and gave her the boost she needed. So Ari played the game and things were fine—at least up until a few weeks ago, when Molly began to seem uncomfortable and nervous whenever they shared an intimate moment. As long as the talk remained benign—about work or current events—Molly relaxed. And sex was never an issue, she thought with a smile. Molly was the most capable lover she'd ever known.

She imagined things had changed because there was only one thing left to say. They had reached the apex of familiarity, their family histories explored, their pasts explained and their individual idiosyncrasies accommodated. She knew Molly cared only about her piano and nothing else she owned, and Molly had learned she was meticulous about everything. And now they sat on the ridge between dating and permanent commitment, and she sensed Molly wasn't sure whether she wanted to move forward. In fact, Ari wasn't entirely sure either. So they remained in this constant holding pattern, but she knew something had to change soon.

The front door closed and she heard Brian and Lynne's voices greet the Nelson parents. She wondered if any fireworks were in store, since Brian and his father battled over most subjects posed at the Nelson dinner table. Brian was the true black sheep, and although this was *his* birthday, Ari wasn't sure Don would be able to curtail the biting criticism that he often hurled at his youngest son. Molly was always the peacemaker, and despite the friction, Ari knew they loved each other. Don would never do to Brian what Jack Adams had done to her. She joined them and gave Lynne a hug.

"I love your blouse," Lynne said, touching the cotton fabric. "The design is great. Whoever picked that out really knew what she was doing."

They laughed at the inside joke, remembering their recent shopping trip to Scottsdale Fashion Square. Ari couldn't decide what to buy and Lynne had made the decision for her. "Yes, my personal shopper has exquisite taste."

The other adults returned to the kitchen and the family room, leaving Brian and Lynne with her. They grabbed the bottle of wine and glasses before settling on the patio. She curled up on the lounge chair and stared at the couple, cuddling on the swing. They were physical opposites, but their personalities comple-mented one another. Brian looked the part of a rebel, with his long blond hair, earrings and various tattoos. His appearance was a sharp contrast to Lynne, who was the epitome of class in a button-down pinstriped shirt, pressed chinos and brown loafers. Her dark curly hair barely touched her shoulders and framed a very pleasant face that perpetually smiled. She was only twenty-five, but she was the perfect combination of youth and maturity, possessing a bubbly disposition that was tempered by a level-headed mind. It didn't surprise her that Lynne was slated to graduate at the top of her architecture class next year.

Brian grabbed the bottle of wine and refilled her glass. "How's my favorite fellow Libra? I hear your party will be much wilder than this one," he said with a wink.

Her eyes widened and she glanced from Brian to Lynne, who was already laughing. "What does Jane have planned?"

Brian smiled wickedly. "I'll never tell."

She rolled her eyes and sighed, admitting defeat. Jane had apparently sworn everyone to secrecy, and she would just need to pray.

"Hey, don't worry, at least not too much. It's going to be great."

He looked to Lynne for confirmation, and she nodded. "Ari, I think you will approve of most of the festivities."

"*Most?* What about the rest?" She sunk deeper into the lounge. Jane would do whatever she pleased because she was Jane. "I just hope you both aren't totally embarrassed," she said, wondering if after the party she would lose the two best straight friends she had ever had.

Lynne chuckled in response. "Are you kidding? I think it will be hysterical—"

"Shush," Brian warned. "You'll give too much away."

"I'm surprised Jane has any time to plan this party since the whole orchid thing started," Ari said.

Lynne set her wine on the coffee table and frowned. "Don't tell me she got another one."

Ari recounted Jane's orchid troubles, and she was relieved to find that Brian and Lynne shared her cynicism about the meaning of the orchids. They agreed someone might be enamored with Jane and meant her no harm. As they walked to the dinner

46

table, she felt better about sharing her thoughts with them and not worrying Molly, who didn't need anything else on her plate. Dinner was uneventful, and Don only took one swipe at Brian's ego, but a deadly look from his wife brought a quick retraction and the peace wasn't disturbed again.

As Molly ascended the back steps, she heard laughter and not the sharp words of an argument. Either was possible anytime Brian and their father ate a meal together. She took a deep breath and entered, the smell of her mother's fried chicken making her mouth water. "Hey, everybody," she called, dropping her purse on the sideboard. She disappeared into the bathroom, and when she returned, she gave Brian a birthday hug and took the chair next to Ari. "Hi, baby," she said, covering Ari's mouth with a sweet kiss.

"Eww . . ." the kids whined, sending the adults into peals of laughter.

"I hope you're not making some kind of a political statement," Don Jr. said to Kenny.

Kenny cocked his head to the side, a piece of fried chicken grasped in his small hand. "Huh?"

Several of the adults began talking about the meaning of two women kissing in a straight society, but Molly's attention remained focused on Ari, who watched the children intently, amused by their antics. She certainly seemed to enjoy kids. Whenever they visited, she was the one who never tired of reading stories, playing baseball or having tea with the dollies. She wondered if Ari wanted a child of her own, a thought she couldn't fathom. She had not mentioned the subject. In fact there were many subjects she'd delicately sidestepped, too petrified to handle emotional intimacy. Physical intimacy was one thing, and with Ari there were no boundaries, but sharing her greatest fears and vulnerabilities was nearly impossible. She kept those buried deep inside a whiskey bottle. She remained quiet for most of the evening, enjoying her family and her beautiful girlfriend.

"Are you okay?" Ari asked once they had said their good-byes and headed into the night, both armed with leftover boxes from Teddy.

"I'm fine."

Ari gazed at her intently, and Molly hoped her expression was convincing. She couldn't handle all the questions that Ari would pose if she suspected her anxieties had surfaced. Ari naturally tried to reassure her every time she sensed Molly was questioning their relationship, and she found Ari's concern equally annoying and helpful.

She took the easy way out and pulled Ari against her for a deep kiss. "Work was nuts, and I've missed you all day."

"Really?"

"Really."

"Do you want to talk about it?"

"Not now. Maybe later." She walked Ari to her SUV. "So, it's still early. Would you like to go to a movie?"

Ari shook her head. "No, there's nothing I want to see." She took Molly's hand and kissed the base of her palm.

Molly grinned, content to play along. "What about a club? Would you like to go hear some jazz?"

"Nope."

"Bowling?"

Ari smirked. "Too noisy and full of drunks."

She pressed her against the driver's side door and let her hands wander up the front of Ari's blouse. "Coffeehouse?"

"Too public."

"Drive-in?"

"Too outdoors." Ari gasped as her thumb caressed the swell of her breast.

"Then what do you want to do tonight?" she whispered.

"You're definitely on the right track."

Chapter Eight

Sunday, October 15th

9:20 AM

When Ari awoke the next morning, she was alone. The phone had rung two hours before, and Molly jumped out of bed. She frowned, trying to remember what Molly said when she kissed her on the cheek and murmured good-bye—nothing like a Sunday morning of the FBI and missing informants to start the week. She rolled onto her back and gazed at the ceiling. Only hours before she'd had a similar view as Molly kissed her belly and let her lips wander southward. Ari's cell phone chimed, interrupting the memory that was clearly taking hold of her body. She checked the display, hoping it was Molly and dreading to see it was Jane. Given the hour, she doubted Jane was calling with good news.

"Hey, what's up?"

"Okay, now I'm really freaked out. Isabel called me six times last night. She's psycho, Ari."

She sat up in bed and tried to focus. "So what did she say?"

"First, she called to ask me what I liked to eat, you know, for our date. Then she called twice more with her own ideas. I can't even remember why she called the next two times. By then I was a mess."

She quickly calculated in her head. "I thought you said it was six times?"

"It was. The last time was a hangup. I answered, but she didn't say anything. She was probably embarrassed."

"Probably," Ari said to ease Jane's anxiety.

"I don't know what to do. I really don't want to go out with her, but I'm kinda afraid to say no."

Ari ran her hand through her tangled hair and felt the beginnings of a tension headache. "Sweetie, you need to accept the possibility that Isabel is responsible for the orchids. She certainly has opportunity, and I'd say she's definitely infatuated with you, which certainly gives her motive."

"I don't know. I was so sure it was a man."

"Well, you certainly can't date people out of fear. That's really warped. I think you need to have a talk with her. Just be honest and tell her that you don't want to see her."

"But what if you're right and she *is* my stalker? She might come after me with a knife or a gun."

"I don't know what to tell you, honey. If you're this worried, you need to hire a professional. Have someone watch Isabel, or watch *you*, to see if you're being followed." Ari wandered into the kitchen in search of coffee. Ever a darling, Molly had brewed a pot and left a sticky note with a heart on the carafe. "Have you slept with any private investigators?"

"Very funny, Ari." Jane sighed. "Actually, I asked the receptionist at work and she gave me the name of a well-respected lesbian who does a lot of work in the community. She hired her when her deadbeat ex-husband skipped out on child support."

Ari poured a steaming mug of magic and took her first sip.

"Who is it?"

"Biz Stone."

She knew the name. Biz had quite a reputation for enjoying female companionship, and it was very possible she and Molly had spent an evening together at some point in the past. "How well do you know her?"

"If you mean, have I ever slept with her, well . . . maybe. She frequents Hideaway, and I know who she is, but I don't *remember* ever being with her."

"Huh," she added absently between sips.

"I already called her, and she's meeting me for brunch, so I hope you can join us. I'm spending the morning previewing houses with Aspen. She swears she knows *exactly* what she wants now," Jane said sarcastically.

"Maybe you'll get lucky."

"In what way?"

She laughed. Jane's mind never strayed too far from the bedroom. "I mean, maybe you'll find the perfect house and Aspen will want to write a contract." A thought suddenly occurred to her. "What are *you* talking about?"

"Well . . ." Jane paused. "It's just that Aspen has been coming on to me—"

"Excuse me? This woman is not the kind of woman you should date. She's a nut."

"But she's a nut who makes an incredible flan. I went over to deliver some more listings, and she was preparing this divine meal. The smells from the kitchen were intoxicating, and she's really a beautiful woman with an unbelievable body."

"And how would you know this?"

There was a long pause until Jane finally said, "Okay. We've already been to bed. I broke my rule."

"Again." Jane had a rule about dating clients, which was as flexible as the Republican Party's ethics. "So she made flan and you jumped into bed with her?"

"Well, it didn't hurt that she answered the door in this little panty and bra outfit."

Ari shook her head and opened the fridge. Inside Molly had left a bag of Einstein's bagels with another sticky note heart. Her lover was scoring big points now. "Did she know you were coming over?"

"Yeah, I called from my car. You think her little seduction scene was planned? She told me she was just multitasking by cooking and trying on new clothes."

She chuckled. "Of course it was planned, sweetie."

"Oh. Well, anyway, what's done is done. I'll see you at twelve thirty, okay?"

"Okay. And Jane, are you and Aspen planning on seeing each other more often? What are her expectations now that you've slept together?" There was no response from Jane's end, and Ari realized the list of potential orchid-senders could be growing. "Look, you don't have to answer that. I'll see you in a while."

She hung up, hoping Jane was learning that her casual attitude about sex was probably at the heart of this problem. Sometimes she could be so blind, caught up in the easy world of pleasure. And not to recognize that she'd been set up was disturbing. For someone as experienced as Jane, her naïveté about the conniving demeanor of women was surprising, but then, Jane was exactly the opposite. There were never any hidden agendas or head games. She saw what she liked and took it. If she wanted to spend the night with a woman, she propositioned her, and she was always honest about her unwillingness to commit. Still, if Aspen Harper wanted Jane, how far would she go to have her?

Chapter Nine
Sunday, October 15ᵗʰ
10:10 AM

Sundays were always busy at Sky Harbor International Airport, particularly Terminal Four, where US Airways and Southwest Airlines shuttled all of the Zonies from Phoenix to Las Vegas or California destinations. The parking garage was full, all of the weekend vacationers still enjoying the San Diego weather or playing the slots on the Vegas strip. Phoenix officers and FBI swarmed the area, and the poor beat cop assigned to crowd control had his hands full with some irate fliers who wanted their cars back. Molly and Andre flashed their badges and ducked under the tape, watching the crime scene personnel assess the situation.

Connie Rasp stood with the medical examiner, past the open trunk of a dark blue Hyundai Sonata. Molly avoided the car, unsure of what she would see, and instead joined Rasp. "Detectives

Nelson and Williams, I assume you know Dr. Haynes?"

"Good to see you again, detectives," Dr. Haynes said.

Molly glanced at the balding man and nodded. It was certainly unusual to have an M.E. present at a crime scene, but the FBI involvement probably accounted for his presence. "Likewise," Molly replied. She had worked several cases with Fred Haynes and found him to be highly competent and thorough. "So what happened?"

"The better question is what didn't happen," Rasp said. "Dudley Moon was shot, stabbed and beheaded. Somebody was definitely trying to make a point."

Molly felt the guilt wrap around her, threatening to suffocate her. She should have insisted that she tail Itchy. She knew his habits, and he trusted her. That was part of his mistake, apparently.

"How long has he been dead?" Andre asked.

Fred Haynes narrowed his eyes and looked toward the trunk. "I'd say two days, but I'll need to do a full autopsy first. Do you want to see the body before they remove it?"

Andre looked to Molly and she nodded slowly.

"Nelson, it's okay to skip it," Rasp said gently.

Molly could hear the kindness of her words, and she was sure Rasp noticed her reaction to Itchy's death. Yet she didn't want Rasp to think she was weak. "It's no problem." She went to the trunk, steeling herself for the worst, which until that moment had been the hanging of a small child by his meth-addicted father.

What she saw would stay with her for the rest of her life. Itchy's beheaded body had been stuffed in the trunk, his head sandwiched between his legs, a clean bullet hole through his skull. His entire head was the color of an eggplant, and his mouth was open, as if he were trying to laugh. His face was bloated, but she could make out a distinct indentation on his left cheek. She pulled her gaze away from Itchy's face—to the knife plunged through his heart. A piece of paper rested on his chest, the blade fastening the paper against him. In a sick way it reminded her of a child with a note pinned to his shirt coming home from school. A single word written in blood told them everything they needed to know—*TRAITOR.*

Chapter Ten
Sunday, October 15th
10:30 AM

Before trekking out to Greenlawn Cemetery, Ari stopped at Trader Joe's and picked up two beautiful bouquets of carnations, her mother's favorite flower. She had no idea what Richie's favorite flower had been since he had died so young and such subjects were not part of any discussion with a nine-year-old. She knew, though, that Richie had adored his mother, and most likely, if he had been asked, he would have turned to Lucia Adams and parroted any response she gave.

Her monthly visit to their graves wasn't born of respect or guilt, but rather for the sake of connection, a bond that she cherished since she had no one else. She would never forgive her father—not completely. He had pushed her away into an abysmal pocket of fear by disowning her at twenty-one, abandoning her because she was gay. Her mother had been nearly helpless at the time, lost in one of her "episodes," unclear of anything around her. Her entire mental state focused on controlling the pain from the cancer. Her mother had told her it was like staring at the head of a pin, where the slightest shift of attention caused her to fall back into the constant ache raging through her body. Such was her condition when Jack Adams told Ari to leave one evening. It wasn't until three days later that her mother realized Ari was gone. She demanded to see her daughter, who refused to return home. As a result, when Lucia felt strong enough, she divorced Jack Adams and moved to Tucson to live with her sister and reestablish her relationship with Ari, who worked for the Tucson P.D. There she spent the rest of her days until she was returned to Phoenix to lie next to her son.

Ari pulled the SUV to the shoulder and walked down three rows to the matching headstones. She gently placed the pink carnations beneath the markers and stepped back. Although she had memorized the inscriptions long ago, she read the etched words as if they were new, as if they might have changed since her visit last month. Her gaze drifted to the empty marker on the other side of Richie. It bore her father's name, date of birth and, "Love conquers all," a quotation her parents clearly had selected during happier times. All that was missing was her father's date of death, and she knew that as her parents' relationship fell into ruins, her mother would have gladly picked up her and Richie's plots and moved them halfway across the cemetery if it were possible. When her cell phone rang and she saw her father's name on the display, her eyes widened. For the second time in two days he had called her just as she was thinking of him. *Weird,* she thought.

She flipped the phone open and sighed before she held it to her ear. "Hello?"

"Hi," he said. The hesitancy in his voice told her that he was still uncomfortable, but he wanted to be familiar, and he wanted her to treat him as she treated others who knew her intimately, the way a relative or a close friend should be. "Am I catching you at a bad time?"

"No, I'm just out here visiting Mom," she said casually.

"Oh . . . well."

Her lips formed into a slight smile, one she couldn't help. He was flustered and she was happy about it. He had treated both of them so poorly that he deserved whatever he got. "I always visit Mom and Richie once a month." She took great pleasure in uttering Richie's name to her father, since she knew remorse and regret instantly slit his heart. He had never found Richie's killer despite an extensive investigation.

"That's nice," was all he could say. After a long pause he added, "I think it's good you visit."

His sincerity and gentle tone disturbed her, and a pang of remembrance touched her heart, something she did not want to feel. "Why did you call, Dad?"

"Well, I just wanted to check in with you, and say that I didn't like the way our conversation went yesterday. You seemed upset that I wasn't coming."

"I'm not upset."

"Are you sure? You sounded disappointed and I was worried. If it means that much to you, I could come."

"No," Ari said abruptly, thinking of the likely activities that would take place at Hideaway. "Really, Dad. It's okay."

"You're sure?"

"Positive. Look, just send me whatever you want to get me, and I'll call you next week after I get it. Okay?"

There was a long pause. "Well, I'll think about it some more. I'll talk to you tomorrow."

" 'Bye, Dad." Ari clicked the phone shut and frowned. She felt out of sorts and couldn't decide if she was upset, sad, disappointed—or ashamed.

She glanced down at the headstones and realized that she was uncomfortable standing in front of her mother's grave while she tormented her father. Despite their divorce, her mother would never approve.

"Sorry," she whispered and quickly walked back to the SUV. She climbed in and leaned against the headrest. She closed her eyes and pushed the feelings away, certain that when she left the cemetery she would no longer be wrapped in the cloak of her family, which up until a few minutes ago had been pleasurable and soothing.

When she reached Smiley's, she knew she was early and the brunch crowd had not yet claimed the best tables around the large picture windows. She found her favorite one, away from the kitchen and the front door. She ordered an iced tea and looked over her shoulder to find a young woman staring at her from the bar. The woman nodded at the bartender and slid off the stool, heading toward her. She dropped into the opposite chair, placing a messenger bag on the floor beside her. Ari smiled at a soft butch with close-cropped brown hair. She found her attractive but not in a noticeable way. She would easily blend into a crowd and never turn heads. Ari guessed she had not turned thirty, and she was blessed with youthful features. She wore a tight, black Led Zepplin concert T-shirt tucked into her jeans, and she noticed a tattoo on the inside of her forearm, a Chinese symbol. Her overall effect telegraphed danger, but Ari guessed such a judgment would be inaccurate. Her intensity was palpable, and she made no effort to immediately introduce herself, quite comfortable violating standing rules of etiquette.

The silence drove Ari into action, fostered by her good manners and the refined conversation skills that came from years in real estate. "Do I know you?"

"I'm Biz Stone. I believe we're both here to meet Jane." Instead of her hand, Biz reached into her back pocket and offered her a business card.

Ari read the simple black print, *Elizabeth Stone, Private Investigator*, a local phone number listed beneath her name. "Biz," she repeated. "That's a very unique nickname."

She smiled pleasantly and studied the silverware. "And a long story."

"Oh, I'm sorry. I didn't mean to pry."

She leaned back and crossed her arms. "Don't worry about it. Everyone asks me that question, but I only tell the story to people who earn my trust, and considering we've just met . . ." Her voice faded out, Biz apparently not feeling the need or interest to complete an obvious thought.

"Of course."

"I've seen you at Hideaway, and I know Molly, too," she added quickly.

Ari nodded in recognition. She'd just never put Biz's name together with the face, but she was always surrounded by several voluptuous femmes at the bar. "Yes, I knew you looked familiar, but I don't think we've ever been introduced."

"No, we've never met officially, but I've seen you. You're not easy to forget."

The comment surprised Ari, but before she could respond, Jane waltzed up to the table. "Hello, hello." She immediately proffered her hand to Biz, who stood to meet her new client. "You must be Biz. I've heard so much about you."

"I doubt most of it is true."

"Are you kidding? I looked you up on the Internet. You're amazing." She took the chair next to Ari and kissed her on the cheek. "Ari, darling, you do know we are in the presence of greatness. Biz is the premier PI in the women's community. She's only twenty-six, but she's helped so many sisters by working for free with the domestic violence shelters. She helps build cases against the SOBs who beat their wives, and the partners who steal from each other." Jane pointed at Biz. "You're a legend. Don't deny it, and I can't believe you're going to help me."

Biz only nodded and sat down again, clearly uncomfortable with Jane's glowing version of her biography. Jane's gushing ended when Ari's favorite waiter came by and took their order. Ari watched Biz absently rake her hand through her hair while she studied the menu and made her selection. A noise from another table caught her attention, and her eyes quickly flickered over her shoulder. She was aware of her surroundings, never allowing a single picture to dominate her full attention. As a private detective, she no doubt couldn't afford to miss anything. Suddenly Biz's gaze shot toward her, and she blinked in surprise. She'd been caught, and judging from the slow smile that spread across Biz's face, she was sure that Biz had noticed her staring the whole time.

When the waiter left, Jane recounted the details of the orchids and the floral shop odyssey from the day before. "I still think it's a man, but Ari thinks it's a woman," Jane said. "What's your opinion?"

Biz looked away toward the bar. "Either of you could be right about the sex, but I don't think this is a random person who's targeting you. That would be highly unlikely."

Jane grabbed a breadstick and began breaking it into fourths on her plate. "So you think my stalker is someone I know."

"Don't you think *stalker* is a bit over the top?" Ari interjected. "You've gotten flowers. It could be someone who really likes you, not someone who wants to harm you."

"You're probably right, Ari," Biz agreed. "But stalkers are dangerous in their own way because they can become angry if they don't believe their feelings are being returned."

"Exactly," Jane said. "That's why I'm hoping you can sift through my acquaintances and narrow down the suspects."

Ari snorted loudly. "And how long are you hiring her for? The rest of your life?" Jane scowled and smacked Ari's shoulder. "Sorry, Jane." Ari turned to Biz to explain. "It's just that Jane knows so many people."

"In the carnal way," Jane said. "You can just say it, honey. Biz knows all about my history with women, and she knows her job won't be easy. Personally I still think it's a guy, but if it's a woman, then I think Isabel is the one sending them."

Ari nodded at the possibility and looked at Biz, who had removed a notepad and pen from her leather messenger bag. Her hands were nicely sculpted, and Ari quickly noticed she wore

61

no ring. *That doesn't mean anything*, she thought. *And why do you care?*

Jane's cell phone chirped, and Ari and Biz listened as she attempted to answer questions for a mortgage banker over the din of the noisy restaurant. Realizing that she was screaming into the phone, she stood up and headed for the exit.

Ari wiped her palms on her pants and turned to face Biz, who continued to stare. "So, Jane says you're a real estate agent, too."

"Yes, but we don't work for the same company. I work for Southwest."

"Oh, you work for Lorraine."

Ari could tell by the way Biz said Lorraine's name that she approved of her. "She's a great lady."

"The best," Biz agreed. "I did some work for her a few years ago. I don't think I've ever met anyone with that much energy. That woman is totally Type A."

They both laughed and continued to smile, even after the small talk had evaporated. Biz leaned back and glanced around the restaurant. She was working, scanning the faces, looking for anyone who was watching Jane as she paced outside in front of the bay windows, obliviously chatting on her phone. Ari realized that unlike Biz, Jane was totally unaware of anything around her. Someone could come up behind her with a butcher knife and she wouldn't know it. There was no denying she was gorgeous—to men *and* women. Even the gay men who walked past her into Smiley's nodded approvingly at her shapely tailored suit and curvaceous figure.

"I guess she's really not my type," Biz said.

"And what is *your* type?" The words spilled from Ari's lips without any thought. She couldn't believe she'd uttered them. Biz would think she was flirting. There was no other way to take the comment, and her face flushed. "I'm sorry. That was inappropriate." She looked away, but she knew Biz was studying her, just as she had done with every other patron in the restaurant.

62

"At one point I thought *Jane* was my type, but apparently she doesn't remember our evening together."

"You and Jane?" Ari shouldn't have been surprised, considering Jane's reputation, but she couldn't believe Jane would have forgotten someone like Biz.

Biz held up her hand. "It was a moment of weakness back in August. Even if Jane doesn't remember it, I do. I was drowning my sorrows at Hideaway after an important client dropped me and refused to pay my fee. Jane was two stools down and started buying me gin and tonics. That's how the evening began. Within an hour I'd forgotten my troubles and she took me home." She leaned close, as if she was going to whisper a secret. "She is incredibly charming, don't you think?"

Ari could only nod, amazed that Biz remembered so many details from a single encounter that occurred a few months before. The waiter brought their plates and she immediately dove into her Caesar salad, grateful for the opportunity to do something with her mouth other than flap her jaws and embarrass herself in front of Biz. Only when Jane returned did she dare to speak, and then only when Jane asked her a question or wanted her to verify that she was telling Biz everything she needed to know.

At last their meal concluded and the bill was paid. They walked out together and stopped in front of Biz's antique, red Mustang. Ari didn't know much about cars, but she thought it was called a Shelby, and she knew those were incredibly expensive. Biz handed Jane a business card. "Call me if you think of anything. I'll see if there are any other florists to check out, and I'll probably tail you tonight when you're on your date with Isabel."

Jane rolled her eyes. "At least I convinced her to let me meet her at Vincent's."

"That was smart of you," Biz said. "With everything going on, you don't need that woman going to your house."

Ari's attention was drawn to the roar of an engine starting in the back lot. A red Dodge Viper whipped out of the parking spot, veering just close enough for her to catch a glimpse of the driver, whose long strawberry-blond hair tumbled around her face. She wore dark sunglasses, but Ari was rather sure it was Aspen Harper.

"Jane, look over there." Jane and Biz dropped their conversation and watched the Viper pull toward the exit. "Isn't that Aspen's car?"

"It could be. That's what she drives."

"I got a pretty good look at the driver, and I think it was her."

"Aspen Harper? That's one of the names you gave me, right?"

"Yes, she's one of my clients, but I doubt she's the stalker."

Biz raised an eyebrow. "Why would you say that? At this point most everyone you know is a suspect. Did either of you notice her inside?" They both shook their heads and Biz looked around. Together they walked to where the Viper had parked and studied the area. Ari noticed that only two doors faced them, a back door into Smiley's and the entrance to a men's gym. "That's the only other tenant on the property, so either she's pumping iron in a testosterone joint, or she left Smiley's by the back door, which normally isn't for customers."

"Maybe we should go check it out," Jane said.

"No," Biz disagreed. "That's why you've hired me. I've got an appointment in ten minutes, but when I'm done, I'll come back here and get some answers."

They walked back to the pristine Mustang and Biz slid inside. Ari noticed that Biz fit in the car the way a fabulous dress clung perfectly to a svelte body or the right perfume smelled magnificent on the shoulders of a beautiful woman. Before she put the car in reverse, she gazed at Ari and then sped out of the lot, looking as cool as she really was.

Chapter Eleven

Sunday, October 15th

5:25 PM

Oaxaca's was nearly deserted when Molly, Andre and Rasp claimed three stools at the bar. The décor was predictable and simple—a stucco interior painted in Southwestern earth tones. Worn black vinyl booths lined the walls, and sombreros and colorful Mexican flowers adorned the entryway. Strains of mariachi music echoed throughout the three dining rooms and bar area, as if to scream authenticity. Diners often shouted to be heard, but the regulars, many of whom were Phoenix police officers, didn't seem to care.

It was the city's cop hangout and memorabilia from the last fifty years decorated the place. In the lobby was a wall honoring the fallen brethren, and police officers would bring in framed photos of their friends receiving citations for display over the semicircular booths. Next to Hideaway, Molly felt most at home at Oaxaca, as it defined the other side of her personality—cop. She was well-known as a good tipper, and Miguel, the bartender, had her Scotch ready before she sat down.

"I take it you're a regular here?" Rasp asked.

"She buys Miguel a Christmas present," Andre said.

Molly glared at him, not wanting Rasp to think she spent her life in bars, which was only a step away from the truth. "All the cops come here, not just me. Right, Miguel?" The bartender nodded at them and took their order. She fired another glare at Andre, who looked down at his shoes.

Miguel brought Andre and Rasp's drinks and a bowl of chips and salsa for them to share. As usual, no one felt the need to plunge into polite conversation until the somberness of the day washed over them. The investigation had stalled with Itchy's death. Molly couldn't stop blaming herself, and at one point during the afternoon, Rasp had leaned over and squeezed her shoulder—an innocent gesture that sent a surge of electricity through her body. She'd shown no emotion and a vision of Ari in a teddy instantly squashed her libido. She was committed to Ari, and now she was feeling a little guilty about sitting in a bar with her partner and an attractive FBI agent rather than accompanying her girlfriend to their regularly scheduled Sunday afternoon activity, a movie at the Orpheum Theater. She knew Ari would understand and would tell her not to feel guilty because she didn't have a jealous bone in her body. Eventually Molly was sure that Ari would meet Rasp, and she would probably recognize the sexual energy between them—and she'd laugh. It had happened before, and she couldn't understand it. How could Ari be so secure in their relationship while she was a wreck?

"Where do we go from here?" Andre posed the question she wanted to ask, but she didn't want Rasp to think she couldn't formulate a game plan. She was, after all, the ranking detective and Andre's superior. Yet she wasn't sure what they could do to make another connection to Vince Carnotti. She knew Rasp would return to New York if none of the leads in Arizona panned out, and Molly found herself thinking harder to avoid that outcome.

Rasp swirled her Chardonnay. "We don't have a lot. The weapon is missing."

"No surprise there," Molly said. "It's probably at the bottom of Tempe Town Lake. Whoever killed Itchy is a pro. He's not going to make mistakes. I'll bet there weren't any prints on the car either."

Rasp shook her head. "Nope. And we checked out that bus pass that belonged to LaDonna Jones. That's another dead end. She's a postal employee who works downtown and lost it a few weeks ago."

"So, I'll ask my question again," Andre said. "Where do we go from here?"

Rasp replied, "We go on that slip of paper you guys found. I agree that Itchy hid those numbers for a reason. We just need to figure out what they mean."

Molly sipped her Scotch and thought about the slogan "Here to Help!" "I already Googled the phrase on the Internet and, as you might imagine, there were pages and pages of hits. It could take us years to figure it out."

"I think we need a different angle," Rasp said. "I'd investigate the paper. We need to find the printer."

"That could be a total dead end," Molly argued. "We could sift through thousands of invoices, and there are hundreds of printing companies in Phoenix. For all we know, whoever printed it already went under."

"You're a bit of a pessimist, aren't you?" Rasp gave a crooked smile and she blushed.

"We've gotta try," Andre said. "It's our only lead. Let's start with the big places tomorrow and work down." He checked his watch. "I've gotta go. I'll see you tomorrow, Mol." He threw some bills on the bar, nodded to Rasp and left.

Suddenly the situation seemed more intimate, and Molly felt guilty, as though she were doing something inappropriate. She reminded herself that she was sitting in a bar with a colleague—

nothing more. The fact that Rasp was extremely attractive, and her chocolate brown eyes incredibly soothing, didn't matter.

"So, are you on board with the game plan, Nelson?" Rasp asked. Her gaze focused on the inside of her wineglass.

Molly's mind jumped back to the investigation. "Yeah, it's all we've got. But I've been thinking about something else, too."

"What's that?"

"Who tipped off Carnotti's people about the operation?"

Rasp shrugged. "There are lots of possibilities. Carnotti is highly connected. My bet is your friend Itchy. I think whoever grabbed him had been following him. He may have tried to bargain for his life. I don't know."

Molly frowned. She had trouble believing Itchy would talk. He'd always been highly reliable and careful. Her concern was on the other end. "You don't think there could have been a leak?"

Rasp shook her head. "I doubt it. I mean, is it possible? Yeah, it's possible. But I've worked with my people for nearly two years. Everyone's put their life into nailing Vince Carnotti."

"I wasn't thinking of your people. I was thinking of mine."

Rasp glanced at her and their eyes met. "Somebody in particular? Someone you don't trust?"

Molly chuckled. "There are lots of cops I don't trust. I've heard rumors about dirty ones, but none of them have anything to do with this investigation. I guess I'm just naturally suspicious, too."

"Why?"

"I'll bet you can guess. It's hard enough being a female cop, but being a lesbian has been really difficult. I get a lot of jokes and I could write a book on sexual harassment."

"You should report it."

"To who? My captain? He's one of the biggest homophobes on the force. He hates me. The best thing I can do is ride out my time until he gets a promotion or I do."

Rasp touched her arm, and Molly's gaze instantly dropped to her hand. She made no effort to remove it. "I know it's hard.

The FBI isn't any different. The good-old-boy network doesn't include me."

"And when have you filed a complaint, Agent Rasp?"

Rasp shrugged. "Look, Molly, we're in a tough position. We're women, we're gay, and we're in a career filled with men. We do what we need to do to fit in and advance. Who wants to be isolated?"

"You're gay?" Molly's jaw dropped and she instantly tried to recover. Rarely did her gaydar fail her, but she never would have pictured Rasp at a pride parade.

Rasp smiled slightly and hopped off the stool. Her eyes wandered up and down Molly's body. "Yes, I'm a lesbian. And we're both taken."

Chapter Twelve

Sunday, October 15th

6:40 PM

Once the movie credits ended, the house lights ensconced the old theater in a warm glow and drew the patrons back into the real world. Ari watched the moviegoers around her hustle to the parking garage, but she was in no hurry. She allowed herself an additional few minutes to stare at the magnificent stage and proscenium of the oldest theater in Phoenix. It was actually Molly who had discovered that the Orpheum showed movies on Sunday afternoons, and they enjoyed ending their weekend with a huge bucket of popcorn and a black-and-white classic. The silent movies were especially entertaining when the grand pipe organ played along with the action. Sitting in the quiet of the theater after everyone else left was their ritual, and although Molly was stuck at work today, she encouraged Ari to go downtown for both of them.

Ari's fascination with the old theater preceded her relationship with Molly. She remembered her parents bringing her to the Orpheum to watch Broadway plays as a kid. Her favorite was *Annie*, and she glanced toward the sixth-row center, at the seats where she had sat with them as they remained mesmerized for two and a half hours by the incredible singing and dancing. At one point, her mother had become fraught with emotion and began crying. Ari remembered her father reaching for his handkerchief and handing it to his wife. A year later their lives would again bend to fate and tragedy would strike—her mother's cancer.

The sound of the ushers talking and sweeping told her it was time to leave. Molly would be sorry she missed *To Have and Have Not*. It was one of their favorite Lauren Bacall movies. On a whim she decided to stop at the store near Molly's apartment and buy the DVD. The two of them could watch it later, snuggling in bed. She checked her watch. It was almost seven, and Molly wouldn't be home for at least another hour. She decided to swing by Jane's apartment and try to catch her before her date with Isabel. She was curious to know if Biz had learned anything more about Aspen's visit to Smiley's.

She was certain that Aspen had been spying on Jane, but the question was why. As she made her way down the freeway, she considered the possibilities. The obvious reason was that Aspen, like so many other women, had succumbed to Jane's sexual charms, which were rumored to be legendary. Although Ari had no firsthand knowledge of Jane's bedroom, she'd overheard enough conversations inside the Hideaway bathroom to know that Jane was revered for her ability to create carnal pleasure. If Aspen wanted more than a good time in bed, though, she would be disappointed, and perhaps she already recognized that and was seeking revenge.

Ari frowned when she pulled up in front of Jane's condo. The lights were out, which meant Jane had already left for her evening with Isabel. She pulled out her phone and dialed Jane's cell.

"What?"

"Is that the way to greet your best friend?"

"I'm getting pissed. We were supposed to meet at seven and Isabel's late. I've already been here fifteen minutes, and she's not answering her cell phone. She made such a big deal about this date."

"She might just be stuck in traffic. She's not *that* late. Give her at least fifteen more before you give up on her."

Jane swore under her breath. "I hate that I'm wasting Biz's time. She's on the clock."

"So she's with you?"

"At least I think she's out there somewhere. We're both just waiting."

She glanced at the condo and noticed the glow of Jane's back porch light spilling over her patio gate. Although she could only see the front and right side of the condo from where her car was parked, she had not noticed the light before. Was it on when she pulled up?

"Jane, did you leave your back porch light on?"

"Um, no. It has one of those motion sensor thingies on it. Teri installed it. It's only supposed to come on if someone's there. Why?"

"Because it's on." Ari slipped from her SUV and started walking up the front path. "I'm going to take a look."

"Ari, you be careful. If anything happens to you, Molly will shoot me, and I'm not being melodramatic."

She knew there was some truth to Jane's words, and she paused at the top of the sidewalk near the front door. She thought she heard a sound—the sound of metal scraping metal. She turned abruptly, dropping her cell phone onto the hard cement. It skittered a few feet away, dislodging the battery from its cradle and disconnecting Jane. She quickly gathered the pieces and circled behind the condo, but no one was there. No cars lingered in the nearby stalls, and the patio was undisturbed, the fashionable chaise longue and table in their usual places. Her gaze swept the parking area. She was alone. Her heart was racing. She took a breath and looked down. The gate latch rested at an angle, as if it had been shut carelessly when someone left in a hurry.

By the time she arrived at Molly's apartment with a copy of *To Have and Have Not*, Molly was home and beautiful piano music poured outside. She smiled and paused with her hand on the knob, enjoying Molly's talent. She recognized the tune as her continual composition in progress, a tribute titled *Aria*. She rested her head on the door and closed her eyes. She knew each measure was Molly's true voice, proclaiming her love in the way that was most meaningful to her.

"It's really coming along."

Ari turned to see Molly's elderly neighbor puttering toward her own door with her grocery cart in tow. "Hello, Mrs. Lyons. You're absolutely right. It sounds wonderful."

Mrs. Lyons's hand shook as she stuck the key in the knob. The short woman with the white hair appeared frail, but Ari knew that her mind was still sharp and she missed very little. "You know, she works on it even when you're not here. Some nights she stays up late practicing her song."

Ari beamed at the thought. "I hope she doesn't keep you awake."

Mrs. Lyons waved her off. "I love it. Besides, once I'm down, I'm done. That's the great thing about being old. You can't hear anything, and you know what, I don't think I'm missing much. But I do like your girlfriend's music."

She was pleased to hear Mrs. Lyons refer to her as Molly's girlfriend, and she grinned. "I do, too."

"You take care, Ari," Mrs. Lyons said. "I've got to take my Metamucil. Another joy of old age. I'll bet you can't wait."

She laughed and watched her disappear into the apartment that smelled of medicine and liniment. The old lady was a kick, and Ari loved talking with her. She decided to invite Mrs. Lyons to dinner some night. She was sure Molly would agree, because Molly had adopted Mrs. Lyons long ago and was always doing little jobs for her around her apartment.

Molly didn't notice her slip inside and latch the door. She had already changed into a T-shirt and sweatpants, a Scotch on the rocks poised on the top of the piano. Ari noticed the glass was half empty, making it difficult for her to gauge Molly's mood. The alcohol was always a signal. If the glass was mostly full, and the bottle was still in the kitchen, her day was decent, but if the bottle rested on the piano along with a glass, she knew she might as well turn around and go home, for the evening was already a disaster in Molly's mind, and no amount of cuddling or fondling could reverse her collision course with pessimism. They never spoke of Molly's drinking, and although she worried about it constantly, alcohol was a taboo subject. Occasionally she'd remind herself that a healthy relationship was built on strong communication, but the drinking issue nagged at her mind until she swatted it away.

She slowly walked to the sofa, her eyes on Molly, watching the fingers sail over the keys, barely touching them. Molly was so gifted and made it look so easy. She looked up and smiled.

"How long have you been here?"

"Just a few minutes." She stretched out on the couch and closed her eyes, immersing herself in the music until it cocooned her. She didn't even notice that Molly had stopped playing and joined her.

"You're half asleep," Molly said, her fingertips stroking her cheek.

Her eyes fluttered open and she gazed at Molly's beautiful face. "I'm just so relaxed. Your music has that effect on me."

"Maybe I should make a CD and market it as a stress buster."

"You could." She knew Molly was entirely kidding. The detective played music only for her, and while she wished Molly would share her talent with the world, she selfishly enjoyed the individualized attention.

Their bodies quickly collided, and they began undressing each other with the leisurely assuredness of experienced lovers, one that promised eventual fulfillment. They often made love half-dressed, because Molly particularly enjoyed Ari's choice of undergarments, and she relished the sight of her in a lacy bra with the clasp undone. Molly had said she got the best of both worlds—a view of her in sexy lingerie and a chance to touch the rich olive skin beneath it.

Just as Molly was about to feast on her nipples, they heard the annoying chirp of Ari's cell phone. "God, I hate those things," she snarled, handing it to her.

Before Ari answered, she kissed Molly deeply. "We're not done yet," she whispered. She glanced at the display and saw her father's number. She sighed and flipped open the phone. Why did he keep calling?

"Hi, Dad," she said, trying to be pleasant. Ari rose from the couch and went to the kitchen, haphazardly buttoning her shirt in an attempt at long-distance respectability with her father.

Molly watched her pour a glass of wine and smiled at the sight. Ari had not bothered to button her pants or fasten her bra underneath her mostly open shirt. She was totally turned on. She went to the piano and played softly, watching Ari pull out vegetables from the fridge to make a salad.

"Dad, really, it's okay. I'm fine either way. We don't need to keep debating it. You're not ready to visit, and I get it. Honestly, I'm probably not ready either."

Hearing the strain in Ari's voice, she glanced up. Ari deftly chopped carrots and tossed them into the bowl. Molly loved watching her in the kitchen. She was so graceful, each stretch a economy of movement, full of purpose.

"Look, Dad, if you want to come down, great. We'll go to dinner and you can meet some of my friends." Suddenly expression changed to exasperation. "No, Dad. Just because I'm a lesbian doesn't mean I need to have sex every minute of my life. You can be here, and I won't be missing out."

Molly shook her head in disagreement and went to Ari, who placed an index finger over her mouth before she could protest.

"Seriously, Dad. Look, I have to go. So you'll just have to decide. No, I don't want anything for my car, and I would have no idea what to do with a metric tool set. I have to go now. 'Bye."

Ari sighed and disconnected the call. She dropped the phone on the counter and pulled Molly into a sizzling kiss.

Molly jerked away, frowning. "Do we need to talk?"

"Nope, we're not having a fight right now," Ari said. She pushed her against the Formica. "I was just kidding about what I said. He'll never agree to come, and then I will get the hot sex that I'm expecting on my birthday."

Molly raised an eyebrow, glanced at Ari's hair and pulled the clip out that secured the loose bun. The soft, dark strands fell against her incredible face and she smiled seductively. Molly slowly stripped Ari's shirt and bra away from her shoulders. "What about right now? You owe me."

Chapter Thirteen
Monday, October 16th
2:45 AM

After an hour inside the parked vehicle, she finally felt a slight chill and hugged herself. It wasn't cold in Phoenix yet, fall never was, but without a jacket, the early morning made her shiver, and it reminded her of the horribly cold Vermont winters she endured as a kid. She tapped her shoes on the floorboard in a syncopated rhythm, attempting to alleviate her growing boredom. Music drifted through her brain, a random remnant of childhood and the Saturday nights when her mother would click on *The Lawrence Welk Show*, take her by the arm and twirl her around the regal living room, bypassing the expensive furniture and antiques. It was a regular event, and she had learned to waltz before she was twelve.

Even then her mother was old. She had not expected to have a daughter at thirty-seven, and when her husband's midlife crisis left her with a pile of debt and a vacant garage where the Mercedes had once sat, both mother and daughter quickly found jobs, moved into a small house and developed an inseparable and fierce loyalty.

They had been dependent on each other for five years, until the daughter turned seventeen and the fighting began. Her mother was no longer her best friend, replaced by a twenty-seven-year-old woman, a fellow employee at the gardening center where the daughter worked. Her mother grew despondent over their lost relationship, constantly asking her to explain, but of course she could not discuss her aberrant sexual preference with her mother.

All became clear one day when her mother came home early from her job at the tailor shop. She had no idea how long her mother had actually been standing on the basement steps, watching her and her lover fiercely attack each other, seeking to give and receive physical pleasure. It wasn't until they both cried out in pure ecstasy that her mother tore into the room, screaming and waving her fists at both of them. They separated hastily and the lover darted upstairs half-dressed. Her mother turned and tromped back up the basement steps, her hand wrapped around the arm rail for support, her feet barely able to move.

She remained on the couch, smoking a cigarette. She imagined the conversation that would follow—the consequences, the inevitable grounding and loss of privileges. When she finally dressed and ascended the basement steps, she found the door blocked. She pushed hard and found a large square box full of her possessions.

She flipped open the cardboard slats and her life careened down a steep ravine from which it would take years to chart a course of escape. Too numb to confront her mother, she'd picked up the box and walked out the door, relying on fate and the "kindness of strangers," a line she adored from her favorite play, *A Streetcar Named Desire*. Conveniently her mother had thought to add a paperback version to the box. She was seventeen. She was on her own.

She tapped her feet again, unwilling to start the engine and draw attention to her vehicle. She didn't want to be noticed, and she'd almost been discovered by Ari a few hours ago as she'd tried to leave a present for Jane on her pillow. She knew Jane kept her spare key under her front flowerpot, and she was terribly tempted to jump from her car, grab the key and run into the house, but she didn't dare. It was nearly three o' clock in the morning, and Jane was back in her own bed, sound asleep—once again leaving a lover without saying good-bye. She'd have to save her present for another day. She lifted the flower from the nearby seat and twirled the orchid gently between her fingertips, watching the petals blur into a wheel of white.

Chapter Fourteen

Monday, October 16th

8:45 AM

Metal doors slammed shut, and women hurriedly stuffed their belongings into their tote bags and rushed out of the YMCA locker room. Ari and Jane leisurely chatted while they changed, enjoying one of the benefits of self-employment. While other women scurried to beat the clock and answer to their bosses, they only answered to themselves. They also lived with an unpredictable housing market that could prevent them from seeing a paycheck for several months and health insurance premiums that were unbelievable.

"So what happened last night?" Ari asked.

Jane shrugged and rolled her stocking up her calf. "Nothing too incredible. Once Isabel finally got there, we ate and went back to her place."

"Did you stay there the whole night?"

Jane grinned. "Well, most of it. I left around one."

Ari watched Jane, noting her carefree attitude, which was surprising considering her previous anxiety over Isabel's proposition.

"Izzie's okay. She's just lonely."

"How did she react when you left?"

Jane looked at her and frowned. "I didn't tell her. I just slipped out while she was sleeping."

Ari chose not to voice her disapproval, but she remembered the crooked patio latch and the sound she'd heard, and she suddenly felt uneasy. Jane had said that nothing was out of place, and she didn't find another orchid, but Ari wondered if she'd interrupted the stalker when she stopped by.

"Jane, how late was Isabel?"

"Really late. Nearly an hour. She was courteous enough to call right after you cut me off, but she didn't get to the restaurant until nearly eight."

Ari thought about the time frame. If Isabel was the one at Jane's condo, it would have taken her roughly twenty-five minutes to cross from Tempe where Jane lived to Central Phoenix and arrive at Vincent's. "How did she act when she got there? Did she say why she was late?"

Jane cocked her head to one side. "You know, she was really out of breath. I thought she had been rushing. She just kept talking about this inconsiderate client who wouldn't leave the shop."

"Her shop's open on *Sunday*?"

She shook her head, unable to answer. "I talked with Biz early this morning, and she's checking out some other florists today."

"Because they weren't open on Sunday. I think Isabel lied to you, Jane."

They grabbed their gym bags and headed for the parking lot. "I've got a huge day," Jane said. "I'm meeting a new client for breakfast, Aspen for lunch and the manager of Hideaway after dinner. She and I are finalizing your birthday plans. *Ciao!*"

81

She kissed her on the cheek and sashayed off toward her Porsche, while every man and a few women ogled her as she passed. Ari realized that Jane was magnetic and totally oblivious to the effect. What she had not told Jane was that her anxiety was growing. After the incident at the condo, she was beginning to agree with Biz that the orchid-sender was a true stalker, someone who may wish to harm Jane for a past snub.

She dropped her gear into the hatch of the SUV and pulled out her PDA. A few taps on the screen revealed a low-key day with much paperwork and little interaction with clients, except for an introductory meeting late in the afternoon. While the slow market afforded her more time to work on Jane's problem, she wished she had more clients. Fortunately, she was a saver, and she had quite a nest egg to get her through the rough economic times. She checked her cell phone, and a flashing envelope signaled a voice mail from Biz Stone. Would she be available to check out the florists with her? She couldn't understand why Biz would need her help, but she calculated the paperwork would only take an hour before her meeting.

Biz answered on the second ring. "Stone," she said simply.

"Hi, Biz. It's Ari. I'm available to go with you, but I'm curious as to why you've asked me."

Biz cleared her throat. "Hold on one sec," she said. Ari heard muffled voices and the slamming of the door. "Sorry about that. I just think it would be helpful to have someone tag along who knows Jane really well and might notice if there's a connection. Those flowers have to be coming from someplace, but if the stalker is growing them or ordering them online, then this is all a waste of time."

"Why not ask Jane to join you?"

"Because I'd rather ask you."

She was momentarily speechless as Biz's blatant flirtation echoed in her ears.

A slight chuckle followed. "Look, if I ask Jane, it will turn into an all-day thing. I don't have time to do the latté circuit, you know?"

She laughed. Biz was a professional, and Jane certainly wasn't when it came to any activity outside of real estate. "Okay. Where shall we meet?"

"At your office? I'll pick you up in an hour."

She agreed and drove to work, thinking she could at least put her desk in order before she left. A call to Molly went straight to voice mail, and she gave up hope of ever having a lunch date with her until her big case was closed. She would not see her again until tomorrow night, as they tried to follow an agreed-upon schedule during the week. They had decided to be together on Tuesdays and Thursdays, with the understanding that the weekends were always spent in either Ari's condo or Molly's apartment. It was an arrangement that provided the distance Molly still needed, but the consistent structure conveyed a quiet commitment to monogamy that they both wanted.

By the time Biz appeared in her doorway, she was answering the last of her e-mail. "Hey," Biz said with a smile.

Her stomach flip-flopped at the sight of Biz, dressed in a Green Day T-shirt and tight black jeans.

Biz looked around the office. "Nice digs. Are you ready?"

She nodded and followed Biz out to the Mustang. For a forty-year-old car, the inside was pristine, and the leather smelled sweet. "This is amazing. It's a Shelby, right?"

Biz raised an eyebrow, evidently impressed. "Very good. It's a nineteen-sixty-seven Shelby GT three-fifty."

"Do you show it?" Ari asked, thinking that it was the most luxurious car she'd ever seen.

Biz smirked. "Nah. I don't have time. I just fixed her up for me."

She started the engine and they zipped out of the parking lot. The two shops were located at opposite ends of the metropolitan area, and they decided to go west to Surprise, a booming suburb in the far corner of the valley, before cutting back across the east to Mesa.

"So how long have you been a private detective?" Ari asked as they cruised down Northern Avenue.

Biz glanced at her and took a drag off her cigarette. She quickly blew the smoke through the open window and returned the cigarette outside as well. "Three years," she said.

Ari waited for her to expand on the answer, and when she did not, Ari returned her gaze to the dashboard. Clearly Biz relied on few words, and years of real estate had taught her that some clients did not enjoy small talk. She had learned that at times it was wiser to honor the silence rather than fill it up with endless chatter.

Several minutes later, just as she had decided what she would make for dinner the following night when she saw Molly, Biz pointed to the side of the road. "Have you ever been there?"

She squinted toward a tiny black building that sat on the side of Grand Avenue. A neon tube light announced that it was Trixie's Dive, and she realized it was the oldest gay bar in Phoenix. "No, I've just heard of it."

"Great place," Biz said. "I've spent more than a few evenings shooting pool and making friends."

"So that makes you a regular?"

"Sort of. Your girlfriend spent quite a bit of time there, too." Biz let the remark sit between them, not bothering to explain.

"I'm sure she did." She knew Molly was not proud of her past, which included a string of one-night stands and lost weekends. They rarely talked about her great familiarity with the lesbian bar scene. It was a topic they avoided, just like her drinking. She wished that Molly could give up alcohol as easily as women.

"Hey, sorry. That was a cheap shot."

"I take it you don't like Molly."

"No, she's cool."

Ari decided not to pursue the subject, and they said little else until they pulled into a small parking lot next to a Victorian house, which had been zoned for a business. It was blue with white trim. A low roof, wide eaves and ornamental brackets added to its unique character. A hanging wooden sign painted with a giant marigold and *Cavanaugh Flowers* swung slightly in the light fall breeze. Flowers grew everywhere around the porch, and Ari could see a greenhouse in the back.

When they entered, a bell tinkled above the door. A short, stout woman overdue for retirement stood behind the counter, bundling roses and wrapping them in cellophane. "May I help you?"

The woman's broad smile conveyed true warmth, and Ari suddenly doubted this sweet little shop had anything to do with Jane's orchid dilemma.

Biz nodded and set her hands on the edge of the counter. "Are you Mrs. Cavanaugh?"

"That's me." The woman grinned.

Biz returned the smile. "Well, I hope you can help me. I'm looking for someone who grows rare orchids. Do you?"

Mrs. Cavanaugh nodded proudly. "We do. We have an incredible greenhouse in the back. Are you looking for a specific kind?"

Biz pulled out a picture of the elephant orchid and the woman recognized it immediately. "Yup, we've got it. It's very rare, but I'm proud to say we've been successful."

"Have you sold any lately?"

She frowned and shook her head. "No, there's not much call for these flowers for sale. They're mainly show flowers, and that's what we do with them."

"So no one has come in asking to buy them?"

"No. We haven't sold a single one in a long time."

Biz looked around and glanced at Ari. "I see. What about phone calls? Has anyone made inquiries?"

Mrs. Cavanaugh thought for a moment and shook her head again. "Nope, not that I can recollect."

Biz sighed and stuck her hands in her back pockets, as if realizing the shop was a dead end. "I don't suppose you know anyone named Jane Frank?"

85

"Only Jane I know is my Aunt Jane, and she's been dead for twenty years. Say, what's with all the questions? Normally people just come in here to buy flowers, but I don't think that's your intention, is it, young lady?"

Biz smiled crookedly. "No, ma'am. I'm actually looking for a long-lost friend who grew orchids here in Phoenix."

Mrs. Cavanaugh studied Biz, apparently assessing where the truth began and ended in the story. "Lots of people grow orchids."

"But not this kind," Biz said. "And that's my only connection to this woman named Jane. I don't have a lot else to go on."

Mrs. Cavanaugh eyed her shrewdly. "I wish I could help you, young lady, but I don't know a Jane, and we haven't had any inquiries about our flowers."

"Is this your family business?" Ari thought to ask. "I think I've noticed it here for a long time."

"Twenty years," Mrs. Cavanaugh said. "It belongs to Mitch and me. Anything else I can help you with? Maybe interest you in some daisies?"

Ari and Biz shook their heads and waved good-bye.

Mrs. Cavanaugh watched them go, a slight smile on her face. She had learned long ago how to protect her customers and her employees. She only looked simple-minded. She had no idea what those women were after, but she always knew it was best to keep her cards close to her chest.

"Who was that?" a voice said from the back.

She turned toward the voice. She so enjoyed it when her "adopted" niece came by. "Hi. I didn't hear you come in."

"I just got here. I didn't want to interrupt you."

She snorted. "You're not interrupting. Hell, you would have done better to talk to them. After all, you're the one who grows the orchids."

The younger woman nodded in agreement. "So, what did you

rather benign. There haven't been any threatening notes or phone calls."

Her mind reached back to Jane's conversations with Izzie. "I think there was a hangup, though."

"What do you mean?"

"Jane told me that the night before last Isabel called her six times to plan their date, but the sixth time was a hangup. What if that was a different person?"

Biz drummed her fingers on the table and stared out into the restaurant. "Jane did tell me that she's had several hangups in the last few weeks. She didn't think anything of it, because she gets so many phone calls in a day, that there's usually at least one."

Anxiety crept into her stomach and formed a knot. She was suddenly glad that Biz was working for Jane. When she looked up again, Biz was staring at her.

"A kid gave it to me," Biz said.

"What?"

"You asked me yesterday how I got my name. It was a kid who first called me Biz. My nickname is the reason I went into investigation."

"It sounds like there's a story behind that."

"There is."

"I'd be interested to hear it."

Biz looked at her, as if debating whether to share. She wiped her mouth on her napkin and tossed it on the table. "After my mother threw me out, I came West to a warmer climate. I went to St. Louis and lived with my aunt and her third husband—a real winner. I spent as much time as I could away from the house, and I got a job working at a women's shelter. These were women who had escaped their abusive husbands and were looking for work, making connections with friends or families, just trying to change their lives. Some only lasted a few weeks before they gave up and went back to the violent situation, and others were terrific success stories. One night this woman named Valerie appeared with her two kids, Frannie and Joey. Frannie was four and Joey was about two. The husband was horrible, and he'd done some vicious things to all three of them—I won't go into it. They were there for about a week, and I got to know the kids rather well. Frannie was amazing and very bright. We used to play checkers, and she loved trying to say my name. I mean, for a four-year-old, *Elizabeth* is a lot of syllables, but she got it."

Ari smiled, but Biz's face clouded and tears welled in her eyes.

"One day I came to work and they were gone. The director said Valerie had gone back to her husband. I just had this horrible feeling, and I thought I was going to be sick. I worried about them for the next two weeks, having nightmares, praying they were all right and that they weren't going to be a statistic. I kept going to the shelter to volunteer, hoping they would come back."

"Did they?"

Biz nodded. "Yeah. Like so many women in abusive cycles, when they'd gone back, he was okay at first—feeling sorry, trying to make it right. Then he turned mean again one night after he got drunk, but this time, Valerie fought back. She'd been around these other women at the shelter, and she was starting to stand up for herself." She paused and took a deep breath.

Ari instinctively took Biz's hand. "You don't have to finish telling me this."

Biz turned to her and smiled. "No, I want to. When Valerie yelled at him to stop, it got her a punch in the face—hard. Two of her teeth came out. The kids started screaming, and Frannie was yelling at the dad, jumping on him. He went into this rage, grabbed a knife and cut off part of her tongue."

"Oh, God!"

"It was horrible. The dad had enough sense to call nine-one-one, and of course, when the paramedics came, they called the police and the dad was taken away to jail. The next day when they were released from the hospital, they came back to the shelter. When Frannie saw me, she smiled and then she tried to say my name, but all that came out was Biz. She couldn't make all the sounds anymore. She was so upset that she couldn't say my name, but I told her it was okay. I liked Biz better, and from then on, I made everyone call me that for her. That's when I decided I wanted to help women. If Valerie had been able to show the courts how abusive that asshole was, she might have done things differently. But she felt she was alone. I don't ever want to see another woman treated that way."

Biz gazed into space and Ari said nothing. They paid the bill and Biz drove her back to her office, insisting that she visit the east-side florist alone. Ari acquiesced, certain that Biz needed some space. She went through the motions of the afternoon, meeting her prospective clients and wading into the massive paperwork that sat on her desk, but she was unable to let go of the lunch conversation. Biz had revealed herself, and she felt flattered to have been the recipient.

Chapter Fifteen
Monday, October 16th
2:06 PM

All of the expertise and forensic technology of the twenty-first century couldn't reveal the mystery of Itchy's numbers. The slip of paper had undergone many tests, but only the most basic information was determined. It was twenty-four-pound weight, the standard weight used for stationery, and it could be purchased in any store that sold fine writing paper. A technician dusted for fingerprints, but only Itchy's were clear.

Molly and Andre spent the entire morning combing the downtown area print shops for possible leads, but no one recalled ever having an account with that slogan. They also learned the font was common and the color, powder blue, was a typical choice. Frustrated after speaking with eight different printing companies, they returned downtown after a quick spin through the Pugzie's drive-thru for some hero sandwiches.

They found Rasp sitting at Molly's desk when they returned. She whispered into the phone, and Molly could tell she was talking to her lover. Her entire face radiated pleasure, and she giggled at one point. When she noticed them standing over her, sandwiches in hand, she abruptly ended the conversation and stood up.

"Sorry for taking your space."

Molly shrugged and dropped the sandwiches on the desk. "No problem. We thought you might be hungry." They set up lunch and recounted their unsuccessful morning. "We could put hundreds of man-hours into this and get nothing," Molly concluded.

"Then we need to think of another angle," Rasp said. "My people spent two hours this morning brainstorming the number combinations, looking on the Internet and researching all the obvious possibilities—bank account, safety deposit box, bus station locker—you name it and we tried it. Whatever that number means, it's not obvious."

"Too short for a phone number," Andre murmured. "It could be an address."

Rasp nodded. "We thought of that. And when you index those four numbers with every possible location in the metropolitan area, you get over three hundred hits. We went ahead and cross-checked, but nothing stood out. Besides, if you were writing an address, wouldn't you want to remember the name of the street?"

They couldn't argue with that logic. Molly popped open a ginger ale and asked, "Anything more on the body?"

"Yeah," Rasp said. "The autopsy results came in, and the M.E. confirmed that Itchy was killed by a bullet from a thirty-eight. The beheading and the stabbing were postmortem. And, of course, he was dumped in the trunk and left at the airport."

Molly thought of the puncture on Itchy's cheek. "What about the cut below his eye?"

"That was a punch," Rasp said. "It happened before he died,

but it's hard to know when exactly."

"He didn't have it the day he got picked up," she observed. "It could be tied to the killer."

"Or not," Andre countered. "Street people wind up in fights all the time. Anything on the car?"

"Nope. It was reported stolen twelve days ago," Rasp replied, "from the parking garage in Paradise Valley Mall."

"Definitely professional," Molly said. "This all ties to Carnotti, but we're going to have a hell of a time proving it." She suddenly realized that she'd wolfed down her sandwich in six bites. *She must think I'm some sort of slob*, Molly thought. She noticed Andre and Rasp were slowly chewing their sandwiches, using the meal as a time to relax.

The conversation glided away from the murder and Andre asked Rasp about the culture in Washington, D.C. Rasp recounted her last visit to the Kennedy Center to see Gilbert and Sullivan's *HMS Pinafore*. Molly listened, unsure of how to participate or what to say. She was not good at small talk and floundered in these situations without Ari. Until they had become a couple, she had avoided parties or social events with coworkers or her few friends. She existed on either extreme of the continuum— festivities with her family who knew her well or random hook-ups with strangers who only wanted to know her body, not her mind. Ari changed all of that, unwilling to become a hermit and demanding that they spend time with other couples. Whenever they went out to a party or an event, she kept Ari at her side, and Ari was the one who made introductions or asked questions of strangers.

While Andre and Rasp finished eating, Molly checked her e-mail. She was surprised to find one from George Linkowitz, a detective who detested her and generally avoided any contact. During a briefing a few weeks before, Link arrived late and found that the only seat left was next to her. His face turned white and he leaned against a wall, opting to stand rather than sit next to a dyke. The e-mail subject line simply read *FYI*, with

94

no message—just a photo attachment. She opened the picture, which was fuzzy and overexposed by the lighting. It was Oaxaca, that was evident, and when she looked closely at the people in the photo, two women, she realized that the image staring back at her on the computer screen was Ari—and Biz Stone. Her initial reaction was neutral until she studied the whole picture, which had obviously been snapped by a cell phone. Not only were Biz and Ari sitting close together in a booth, they were holding hands.

"Whatcha lookin' at, Mol?" Andre asked. He leaned over her shoulder and looked at the screen. "Is that Ari?" She said nothing and swallowed hard. He finally added, "Shit."

She wheeled around to face Rasp and gauge her expression. Their eyes met, and Rasp looked down. She was relieved to see Rasp had no comment and chose not to add to her discomfort. She minimized the photo and turned her back on the computer, determined to keep her personal life out of the office.

"So where do we go from here?" Andre asked her, and she threw him a weak smile, grateful for the diversion.

"I think we hit the streets and talk to Itchy's contacts," she said. "Find out if anybody knows anything. I've got several names in my notes that we could follow."

Rasp nodded. "Sounds like our best bet. I'll have the experts keep working on the memo pad and the numbers. Somebody might have a moment of brilliance and come up with the answer." She wadded up her sandwich wrapper and tossed it in the trash on her way out.

Andre looked at her. He knew her vulnerabilities, and she was certain that he had heard about her drinking and her wild life before Ari. Although they didn't spend hours psychoanalyzing each other or sharing intimate details of their lives like some of their brethren, enough was said during their small-talk time— while they canvassed neighborhoods looking for witnesses or sat on stakeouts as they had for the past week. It was the little comments, the pauses in the conversation, the body language and sometimes the anger that showed how well they knew each other. And she knew that Andre was waiting for her to decide whether they kept working or called it a day so she could handle her personal crisis with Ari.

She opted to do a little of both. "Let me send an e-mail while you go get the Wainright file out of storage. Itchy mentioned a lot of people during that case. We'll make a list and see who's around."

Andre left and Molly returned to her computer. She pulled up Link's e-mail and hit *Forward*.

Chapter Sixteen

Monday, October 16th
5:18 PM

Ari checked her watch and saw that she had a few hours before she met Jane for dinner. She decided to finish her e-mail, which had multiplied tenfold during the day while she was out with Biz and meeting with her new clients. Then, she'd spring for her own birthday present and get a massage.

She glanced at her inbox, noticing that thirty-eight messages awaited her attention, and she began prioritizing and eliminating them. The ads and spam she deleted without opening, and she noticed several of the subject lines were about matters that could wait until the morning. Halfway down the string was one from Molly. She grinned, recognizing there was a photo attachment. They were always sending funny pictures or messages back and forth, especially on days when they wouldn't spend the night together. There wasn't a message, which was unusual. She clicked on the picture, and it only took a moment for her to recognize the subjects and the location. She closed her eyes momentarily, angry that Molly's fellow officers could be so cruel. She was aware of the immature pranks and mean-spirited jokes cops played on one another, especially against officers they didn't like. For Molly it was a fifty-fifty split, and anyone in her squad was as likely to give her a break as they were to kick her in the teeth. Whoever had sent her this picture wasn't a friend, and she imagined Molly's insecurities were raging. She saw it as Molly would—as two lovers meeting secretly. She needed to share the truth immediately. The massage forgotten, she punched in Molly's number. After several rings, it went to voice mail. She disconnected and hit redial, assuming Molly was upset and avoiding her, but she wouldn't allow it. This time Molly answered—but she said nothing.

Ari waited, knowing the silent treatment was part of her punishment. After nearly half a minute, she said, "Baby? Are you there?"

"Yeah."

The clipped answer told her everything. "Molly, you need to let me explain. I saw the e-mail, and it's not what you think."

"Well, what *should* I think? Do you want to tell me what the hell is going on, *dear*?"

She closed her eyes and her mouth went dry. "There's nothing to it. Yes, I had lunch with Biz. She asked me to go with her to check out the florists since I know Jane so well. We wound up at Oaxaca, and she told me this very sad story. I took her hand to console her. It wasn't anything."

"It must have been some story. I didn't know you even knew Biz."

"I didn't until the other day. Jane introduced us when she hired her. She was taking your advice."

"And Biz was clearly taking liberties. Ari, that woman is as loose as Jane. And she doesn't care that you have a girlfriend."

"I take it you're jealous."

"Damn right I'm jealous! I don't want my woman anywhere

near her. Do you understand?"

Ari's Italian temper flared at the ultimatum. It was the kind of comment her father typically had made to her mother during one of his jealous rages. "Your *woman*? It's not like you own me. I told you I'm not having an affair, but I'm not going to tell you that I'll never see or talk to her again. She's working on Jane's case, and if she needs my help, then I'm going to give it to her."

"Great! You can do whatever the hell you want. It's not like we've made a commitment to each other."

The comment deflated Ari immediately. Without realizing it, she had balled her free hand into a fist. The tears came at will and she was no longer able to speak. She pressed the END button to eliminate the awful silence between them.

Chapter Seventeen

Monday, October 16th

7:33 PM

Jane dragged her fingers across the rows of hangers in her walk-in closet as she debated what to wear for her dinner with Ari. She was sure Ari would be dressed in a smart pants and blouse ensemble, her standard going-out attire. She also knew that heads would turn at the sight of Ari's long legs and gorgeous dark hair. A touch of envy pricked at her, and she shrugged it off quickly, focusing her energies on selecting something that would rival Ari's natural beauty. Her competitiveness peaked whenever she felt compared to her. She knew she could have any woman she wanted, and she could turn heads when she walked through a room—yet Ari could turn more.

She finished surveying her bedroom closet, unsatisfied with the choices. She headed into the second bedroom to find more options. No guest would ever stay over, since the room functioned as her own department store. Rows of portable clothes racks filled the space, and Teri had designed and built shoe cubbies for each of the walls. The closet served as an accessories area, and she owned enough purses and jewelry to go with every possible outfit she could contrive. She went straight for the most expensive rack, realizing she should have started there. She chuckled at her indecisiveness. Ari did nothing to warrant this competitive streak. If anything, she was apathetic about her appearance and its effect on others. She was oblivious to the stares of strangers and refused to cater to the changing fashion trends.

She selected a crème-colored silk blouse, a short, black leather skirt and a chic pair of pumps that would give her the height necessary to stand near Ari, who would otherwise tower over her five-foot-four frame.

An hour later, she looked in the mirror and was pleased with the results. It only took a few hundred dollars in clothing and makeup to achieve the desired look, but she had acknowledged long ago that beauty was a job for her, whereas Ari woke up with a natural loveliness and needed only to spend a few minutes applying a little blush and lipstick. The doorbell sounded and she glanced once more at the mirror before bounding down the stairs and opening the door to greet—Aspen.

"Hey, honey," Aspen said. She embraced her and pushed her against the open door in one motion. "I've missed you," she murmured before her tongue slid down Jane's throat and her hands stroked her buttocks. "Take me to bed."

Jane gently pushed Aspen away long enough to shut the front door. "Let's not give my neighbors a show."

Aspen shrugged and dropped to her knees. "Why not? Most of them could probably use the education." She hiked up Jane's skirt, pulled down her pantyhose and licked her thighs. "Forget the bedroom. I'm too horny and impatient."

Jane's eyes widened. Aspen's fingers burrowed under her thong and touched gold. "Darling, Ari will be here any moment. I don't have time for this." She gasped. Aspen ignored her comments and thrust her tongue deep inside. She fell back against the wall, realizing it was no use to fight, and she enjoyed it too much to stop her. Aspen was an exceptional lover. She wrapped her hands around the back of Aspen's strawberry blond hair and pulled her against her hips. She watched Aspen's technique in the reflection of her foyer mirror until she was completely satisfied and had screamed, "Oh, God," at least five times. She prayed Ari wasn't waiting on the other side of the door.

"Did you enjoy that?" Aspen asked with a wicked smile. She stood up and kissed her on the cheek. "I know you're going to dinner, but I'd love to see you later."

Before Jane could answer, the doorbell rang. She rushed to the mirror, rearranged her skirt, realizing her face was flushed, and it was highly likely that Ari would know what they were doing.

Aspen chuckled. "Jane, honey, there's no hiding great sex."

She opened the door and frowned automatically. They had known each other too long not to recognize moods, and Ari looked totally dejected. "What's wrong?"

"We had a fight. Nothing new."

"Come in. Aspen was just leaving." She watched Ari's flustered expression as she processed the situation. Aspen smiled broadly and Jane realized the only thing missing was a postcoital cigarette. *I could sure use one*, she thought.

Ari looked at both of them. "God, I'm sorry. Did I get the wrong night?"

"No," Jane said quickly. "Aspen just dropped by unexpectedly and now she's got to go."

"What about later?" Aspen asked as she shoved her out the front door.

"Not tonight," she replied, slamming the door shut harder than she meant to. She took a deep breath, knowing she might have just blown a commission. Aspen would be furious. She turned to Ari and bit her lip. "Sorry."

Ari just shrugged and looked at the floor. "Don't be. At least one of us is happy."

"Trust me. Aspen does not make me happy. Horny, yes, but not happy." She put her arm around Ari and led her to the kitchen. She poured both of them a glass of Pinot Grigio and joined her at the pub table. "So what was it this time?"

She could see the hesitancy in Ari's eyes. "Well," she began with a breath, "Biz Stone called me this morning and asked me to go to the florists with her."

"When did this happen? After we left the Y?"

Ari nodded.

"Why would she want you to go with her? I'm the victim, and I'm single."

She shook her head. "Why is that important? I'm not single, but can't I do things with other people? People who *are* single?"

The frustration in her voice was obvious. "So Molly didn't think you should spend time with Biz?"

"It was a little more than that." Ari told her the story of the afternoon and Molly's reaction, which wasn't surprising.

"Honey, it's clear how Molly feels, and I know you feel the same way. You two are the most obvious couple I know, and now you're frustrated. I'm surprised it's not affecting your performance in the bedroom."

"Well, it's not," Ari said defensively.

She took Ari's hand. "Honey, maybe you just need to say the words first."

Ari snorted in disagreement. "Jane, if I told her, she might self-destruct."

Ari was a goner. She'd fallen hard for Molly, and now she was exercising amazing patience and restraint. Molly was a wonderful person, but she was very complicated. Jane doubted few women would wait so long for a reformed womanizer who was most likely an alcoholic. Secretly she wondered if Molly was worth the effort, but Ari loved her, she was her best friend, and she was a saint.

"Sweetie, what are you going to do? Be honest with me. Do you have any feelings for Biz?"

Ari sighed and swirled her wine. "I'll admit that I think Biz is an interesting person. She's intriguing, but I can be intrigued by a woman and committed to another. I love Molly."

She smiled. Ari was the most genuine person she knew, and she hoped Molly knew how lucky she was. She patted her hand and stood up. "Let's go eat. I'm starving."

"There's a shock. You didn't tell me you got more orchids."

Jane noticed Ari was looking at the extraordinary arrangement of orchids sitting on the dining room table. It was enormous, filled with a variety of flowers in an exquisite crystal vase, including a single *Angraecum elephantinum*.

She grabbed her purse. "Those don't count. That's an arrangement from Izzie. She sent it as a thank you for our night together." She took Ari's arm and led her out. "Now, I don't want to talk about Izzie. I want to focus on whatever you need to talk about to help you patch things up with Molly, and then we'll talk about my problems, of course."

"Of course."

She pointed a warning finger at Ari. "All I know is that the two of you had better figure this out before Friday, and Molly had better behave herself. I've got a fabulous soiree planned."

"Soirée? What kind of a word is that?"

"It means a fancy kick-ass party. And that's what you're going to get!"

Whenever Ari had a fight with Molly, she was reminded about the value of her friendship with Jane. They had so much in common—their careers, issues with their parents, a general fascination with people and their total distaste for phoniness. Yet they were opposites, and the balance added a complexity to the friendship that kept it interesting.

"So tell me more about Teri," she said during dinner. She was sure Jane would change her outlook on relationships if she'd consider someone different.

Jane shrugged. "I don't know that much about her. She came from back East, and none of her people live around here. She spends most of her time working, and she hates the bar scene. She's amazing with anything around the house." Jane glanced up from her swordfish with a raised eyebrow. "Don't tell me you think Teri's intriguing *too*?"

She scoffed at the notion and speared her asparagus. "I wasn't asking for me, Jane. I think you should go out with her."

Jane nearly choked on her swordfish. "I don't think so. She's totally not my type."

"And Aspen is your type? Or Isabel?"

She waited until she had set her napkin back in her lap before answering. "Isabel is a classy lady—"

"Who just might be a stalker. That's a great choice."

"You don't know that she's the one."

"She certainly could be. She was late for your date, possibly because she was waiting for you to leave your condo. Someone was there, Jane. If I hadn't scared her away, I'm not sure what you would have found." The weight of her comments halted the conversation momentarily and Jane focused on her food.

"I suppose you could be right," Jane admitted.

"What's going on with Aspen?"

Jane pointed her knife in Ari's direction. "That's just physical attraction."

Ari shook her head. Jane was talking in circles and logic was nowhere in the middle. "Have you found a place for her yet?"

"We were supposed to go out this morning, but she canceled on me—"

"And showed up unannounced six hours later for sex?"

Jane shrugged. "Maybe she's not serious about buying."

"I think that's a distinct possibility."

"I mean, besides the sex part, she's full of contradictions. You know how most buyers have certain ideas, and they may not have everything figured out, but there are certain features that are nonnegotiable? They want three bathrooms, or a den or a screened porch."

Ari nodded. She knew the type. "So what does Aspen want?"

"That's just it. One day she wants a two-story, and the next day she'd rather have a ranch-style with a basement. I can't win. She is totally indecisive, and I'm beginning to think it's a game."

"Maybe it is. Now that you're sleeping with her, she could be looking for a way to hold on to you."

Jane's face paled at the suggestion. Once again they had returned to the topic of Jane's stalker.

"Did Biz check out Aspen? Does she belong to that gym next to Smiley's?"

Jane snorted. "Of course not, and apparently she's a regular at Smiley's. She comes in a lot, and the bartender can't remember if she came by that day, but it's possible."

Ari reached across the table and squeezed her hand. "Honey, you're playing with fire. Remember that."

They finished their dinner without further mention of the orchids or the stalker by guessing what Jack Adams would purchase for Ari's birthday. They were still laughing at the idea of a weight bench when they pulled into Jane's driveway. Ari sensed something was wrong before they got out of the SUV. By the time they reached the back door, they looked at each other, both aware that something was burning.

"What the hell is that smell," Jane said, ramming her key into the door lock. Nothing in the kitchen was disturbed, and as they headed into the living room, Ari knew they would find a fire in the fireplace. What she did not expect was a sea of white and green. The stems and leaves of orchids were everywhere.

"What the hell!" Jane exclaimed. "Who is doing this?"

"You need to call Biz."

"Damn right."

While Jane paced the room and stabbed at the keypad on her cell phone, Ari picked up a handful of the remains for inspection. What she held were stems and heads of a variety of orchids. Someone had deliberately hacked up dozens of flowers and left them strewn around the living room. She listened as Jane described the scene to Biz over the phone and disappeared into the kitchen. The clinking of glasses suggested Jane was pouring a glass of wine. Ari's gaze immediately went to the dining room table. The arrangement of flowers was gone. She slowly turned toward the stairs. A trail of petals ascended the steps, in the direction of Jane's bedroom. In any other situation it would have been highly romantic, but a weight fell on her shoulders and she dreaded whatever she would find. She climbed the steps and saw the string of flowers turn into Jane's bedroom. The door was shut, and she took a deep breath before opening it.

The flowers ended at the foot of what was left of Jane's bed. She could barely make out the purple pattern of the expensive duvet amid the flurry of down and feathers. Someone had ripped the mattress into tatters with a large knife, and in some places the cuts were so deep that the springs were exposed. She swallowed hard, recognizing that her friend's life was in serious jeopardy, and for some reason, the stalker had turned violent. She guessed the person felt betrayed.

When she could finally pull her gaze away from the bed, she noticed that everything else in the room was untouched, but there was one noticeable addition. Sitting in the center of Jane's wide oak dresser was the orchid arrangement that Isabel had sent. The stalker had placed it in a position of prominence, elevated above the bed, above the destruction. Her stomach turned over, and she heard Jane's footsteps behind her. Before she could shut the door and shield her best friend from the sight, Jane was in the room, too stunned to speak.

"Long time no see, stranger," a voice called.

Molly looked up from the bar toward Vicky, her favorite bartender at Hideaway. She nodded and Vicky placed a Scotch in front of her. "Good to see you, Vic."

"I was missing my favorite tipper. I heard you ditched the

bar scene for Ari Adams." She offered a shrug but no explanation. Vicky smiled knowingly. "But I assume you're here because you and your girlfriend had a fight or you're no longer together. Which is it?"

One answer was right and the other was close, she thought. She drained her glass and set it before Vicky again. She didn't discuss her personal life at the bar. Years of drinking had taught her that it was best not to make friends since you never knew what would come out of your mouth after a few Scotches. Vicky took the hint and silently refilled the glass. Once she had moved down the bar toward friendlier patrons, Molly pulled open her cell phone and checked the call history. Ari had called six times in the last few hours, but apparently she'd given up around nine thirty. She stared at the screen, a sliver of anxiety crossing her mind. She debated whether she should call her back. *What if something was really wrong?*

She dismissed her worries and glanced around the bar. Nothing much had changed in the last six months. Women huddled together, some as friends and others eager to become lovers. She saw the desperation on their faces and knew she had once been one of them—before Ari. All of the regulars were here, except the woman she had hoped to confront. She searched for Biz, and when she didn't see the PI, her anxiety returned.

"Hey, Vic," she called.

Vicky finished making a margarita and stepped in front of her. "Want another?"

Molly shook her head, realizing that what she needed was to go home and play the piano. She didn't want to be in a bar. "Hey, have you seen Biz Stone tonight?"

Vicky looked around, a puzzled expression crossing her face. "That's funny. She was here a while ago." Vicky turned to one of the regulars perched on the corner stool of the bar. "Hey, Sammy! Where'd Biz go?"

"She left," Sammy called back. "Got some phone call and ran out."

Chapter Eighteen

Tuesday, October 17ᵗʰ

9:17 AM

Despite going to bed around two o'clock, Ari awoke and was ready to head out by nine. She looked in on Jane, naked under the guest room covers. Her best friend was now her roommate indefinitely.

When Biz had arrived at Jane's house and assessed the damage, she urged Jane to leave. Ari was surprised at how easily she agreed, vowing to put her place on the market once she could clear it out. The police arrived and took a report, urging Biz to find enough evidence for a restraining order against *someone*. They vowed to patrol Jane's neighborhood diligently, and because Ari was Jack Adams's daughter, she knew they would. Still, she imagined that finding the stalker would fall on Biz's shoulders, a reality that provided comfort and anxiety at the same time. Ari still had not ruled out the possibility that Biz was involved, and she found herself scrutinizing the PI's every move.

Ari reached for her purse and opened the door, nearly running into Biz. "Oh, gosh, sorry."

"Good morning. How's Jane?"

"Still asleep. I'm going off to work."

Biz leaned against the doorjamb and hooked her thumbs into her jeans pockets. "I was hoping I could convince you to help me with this investigation today."

She shook her head, determined to distance herself from Biz. "I don't think so, Biz. I really have a lot to do." She brushed past her and headed for the elevator as her stomach started to churn.

Biz followed behind and touched her shoulder. "Ari, are you angry with me?"

"No, of course not." The elevator doors slid open and Biz joined her for the ride to the lobby. "It's just that Molly's cop buddies saw us together yesterday and didn't waste any time telling Molly. Now she's really upset with me."

"Because the cops thought we were lovers," Biz concluded.

"Probably."

"And that would be a bad thing."

Ari jerked her head around to meet Biz's amused expression. "Biz, listen to me. I love Molly. I do like your company, but if we're going to collaborate or be friends, you can't keep coming on to me. Otherwise, I'm not going to have anything to do with you. Are we clear?"

Biz nodded slowly. "I'm sorry." The door opened and before Ari could step into the lobby, Biz blocked her exit. "I'm sorry if I put you in an awkward position with Molly. I didn't mean to do that, really. But I'm going to be honest with you, Ari. I know what Molly sees in you, because I see the same things. I think you're amazing, but I respect the fact that you're with her. I'll honor that. I won't make any more suggestive comments."

Her face softened and she offered a slight smile. "Thank you."

Biz walked her to the SUV. "Now, I really could use your

help. There are a lot of people to watch, and I'm not sure which direction is the right one. I'm leaning toward Isabel. I get a really odd vibe from her, but Aspen's right there, too."

Ari thought of the night before and the way Jane threw her out of the condo. "I would agree that she's definitely at the top of the suspect list. She's as obsessed with Jane as Isabel is."

"Sounds like it."

"And that orchid arrangement went untouched. It was deliberately moved to be noticed, but why put it there?"

Biz shrugged. "It could be that the stalker just wants to throw us off. Make us think it's Isabel. I don't know. There's a lot I don't know," she added in frustration.

She leaned against the door, wondering if they were missing other possibilities. "Jane has slept with so many people and left their feelings in the dust. Any one of them could be the stalker."

"I guess that would make me a suspect too," Biz said with a laugh.

Biz's expression conveyed nothing, and it seemed as though she had made the remark in jest, but Ari wondered how Biz felt about Jane forgetting the encounter. When Jane had told her she was hiring Biz, she made no mention that she knew the woman or that they had shared a bed. Even when Jane saw Biz, there was no recognition. Could Biz be harboring some sort of desire for Jane? Or a grudge?

"I think we can probably cross you off the suspect list," Ari said, hoping she sounded sincere.

"Thanks," Biz said dryly. "Seriously, if you have any time and could help me research some of these women, it would be great. I'm handling three other cases in addition to this one."

"Okay. I'll see what else I can find out about Aspen, and you work on Isabel."

"Excellent."

Biz gave her a quick peck on the cheek and walked away. Ari shook her head. Biz could turn an innocent gesture into a flirtation, and Ari couldn't decide if she liked it or not.

After two hours of meetings with prospective clients she gained from referrals, she decided the best way to learn more about Aspen was to go to the source. For lunch she headed over to Emerson's, the restaurant where Aspen worked. Ari had never dined there since the prices were exorbitant. Now at least she had a legitimate excuse. She waited until the noontime crowd vanished, hoping someone would have time to talk with her.

She knew from the moment she crossed the threshold that the place was classy. The interior was impressive, resplendent with expensive furniture and plants tastefully displayed throughout. Emerson's had a reputation as the premier dinner spot for yuppies and Ari's initial reaction was that it lived up to it. Every detail from the monogrammed cloth napkins to the crystal highball glasses screamed expensive. She asked the hostess to seat her in the bar area, which was virtually empty. The bartender, a young brunette, was busy restocking after the lunch rush. Every once in a while she would glance toward the last two patrons as they nursed their drinks and watched sports on the muted TV that hung over the bar. Aspen was nowhere to be found, and Ari assumed she was in the back attending to her duties as chef.

The bartender lay a napkin down in front of her and smiled. Ari noticed her nameplate—Elsa.

"What can I get for you?"

"I'd like a glass of your house Pinot Grigio and a bowl of minestrone."

Elsa nodded and went to place the order.

When she returned with the wine, Ari plopped down a twenty, hoping it would buy her some conversation. "So how long has this place been open?"

Elsa thought and busied her hands by wiping the bar around her. "I'd guess about three years, but I'm not really sure. I've only worked here for eight months."

"Do you like it?"

"It's a job. The tips are fantastic on the dinner shift. Lots of rich folks going out."

"But you're not on the dinner shift."

Elsa nodded and frowned. "Not often. That's a seniority thing, and I haven't done my time in the trenches. The owners are really big on rewarding loyalty."

"Well, I've always heard great things about this place. People are always raving about the food."

"And it's gotten even better since Aspen Harper took over the kitchen," Elsa said. "She's an amazing chef. She changed a lot of the recipes that were only so-so, and now there's not a bad thing on the menu."

A waiter came by and set Ari's soup on the bar. One spoonful of the minestrone confirmed Elsa's opinion. "This is wonderful," Ari said. "So I've read that Aspen can be a little difficult to work with. Is that true? Is she one of those temperamental chefs with an ego?"

Elsa wiped down the counter and repositioned the condiments. "I wouldn't necessarily agree. I think the people saying that stuff are the jealous guys who are afraid of a powerful woman. Not that she doesn't have a mean streak," she added. "She's not someone I'd ever want to cross."

"What do you mean?"

Elsa nodded at the two other bar patrons as they got up and left. She looked around before she spoke. "I'm just saying that if things aren't done right, she'll throw a fit. She does have a temper. One time the owner suggested she change some of the ingredients to a sauce, and she came unglued. She yelled at him in front of the entire kitchen staff."

"What did the owner do?"

"Nothing. She's the chef, and he really didn't have any right to question her."

"But it's his restaurant. Doesn't she work for him?"

Elsa raised her index finger, as if to give Ari a lesson. "Yes. However a restaurant is only as good as your chef. If you don't have a great chef, you might as well close your doors. Aspen knows she's a commodity. She could leave anytime and have another job in a second. So Romero, that's the owner, knows to keep her happy."

"And how does he do that?"

"Lately it's been with time off. She's asked for a few nights and afternoons. Romero didn't want to give it to her, but he knows better than to say no."

A red flag went up in her mind. "Why does she want to take time off?"

"I don't know. I think it has something to do with a woman." Elsa leaned close to her and whispered, "Aspen's a lesbian, and I think she's involved with someone. The wine steward overheard her on the phone, and she was saying she was really angry because this woman isn't noticing her. Ever since then she's been acting kinda weird, and the whole staff suspects it's because this woman is on her mind."

"So the other woman doesn't want her. Is that the problem?"

"That's what we think. She's been in a foul mood for the past two weeks, and I'm rather sure it's because this lady friend isn't working out."

"So I take it she doesn't deal well with rejection."

Elsa grinned. "You're right."

Chapter Nineteen

Tuesday, October 17ᵗʰ

3:30 PM

Molly rubbed her temples and glanced at the crumpled sheet of paper. She crossed off another name, another dead end that didn't remember Itchy or couldn't coherently articulate any information. *Such is the life of street people*, she thought. The hangover headache was a steamroller pressing against her skull. She hadn't felt this bad in months—since before Ari, when she spent all of her evenings hunkered over the bar, a glass of Scotch beside her and the bottle just a few feet away. Her life was much better now. Everything was better with Ari.

She would need to think of a way to apologize tonight, but for now she and Andre needed to locate the last name on her list. Only two of the twelve contacts had provided any help at all. Penny, a young prostitute, had seen Itchy talking to some men in suits the week before. When she asked Itchy who they were, he called them his meal ticket. Another street person, Walter, recalled that Itchy had flashed a wad of cash at the St. Vincent de Paul dining hall last Saturday.

Andre leaned against their car and gazed down the street. Molly saw no one, including Rusty, the final contact. "Are you sure he lives here?"

Andre craned his neck toward the building in front of them, a six-story hotel that reminded her of Itchy's place.

"Last known address," she said, checking her notes. "Let's go." She opened the creaky door and wandered into a lobby that reeked of burning incense. She noticed the desk clerk and suspected he was the culprit. She could only imagine what smell he was trying to conceal. They approached him, and he quickly reached for a can of air freshener. Forest pine mixed with incense nearly made her gag. Still in the air was the faint trace of marijuana, which she ignored. She stared at the thin figure, whose long beard compensated for his bald head. He nervously tapped the countertop and forced his lips into a tight smile.

"We're looking for Rusty," Andre said.

The clerk pointed to a figure lounging in an overstuffed chair, his fedora tipped over his forehead. Molly imagined the old man was sleeping, but he'd need to continue his nap later. He was dressed in a trench coat and jeans, a bright orange Phoenix Suns jersey with Steve Nash's number thirteen clearly visible. Several chains protruded from his shirt collar, and she imagined he kept his valuables around his neck.

"Hey, Rusty," Andre said. He tapped the man's foot with his notebook, but Rusty didn't move.

"What?" he asked from under the fedora.

Molly still couldn't see a face, but the voice didn't match what she expected. "Sit your ass up," she said, knocking the hat into his lap and revealing a tuft of blond hair. Her jaw dropped at the sight of a boy. He was young, his face dimpled and white. He was about five-six and of average weight. She pictured him in a baseball cap, not an old man's hat. "How old are you?"

"I'm sixteen," he said. He pulled a wallet from an inside pocket of the coat. "Want to see my ID?"

"Yes," she said, snatching the worn leather billfold from his hand. She carefully studied the picture and the quality of the ID.

"That's real. It's not a fake," he said.

"So why aren't you in school?" Andre asked.

He kept his head down and wouldn't look up. "I dropped out. I hated it."

"Which high school?" Molly whipped the question at him, watching his eyes. He was searching for an answer, and she knew he was a liar. "Don't bother making something up, because I would have asked you to recite your last address, and when the address didn't match with the local high school, I'd know you were lying. Stand up."

Rusty did as he was told, and Molly patted him down before pushing him back on the sofa.

She leaned over him and narrowed her eyes. "Now, tell me again. How old are you?"

His head fell back against the cushion and he closed his eyes. "Fourteen."

She sighed deeply. Many runaway teens settled on the Phoenix streets during winter, but each time she interviewed one or found a child dead in an alley, she couldn't help but think of her niece and nephew—their eyes bright with hope, their futures tucked beside them each night in their comfortable suburban beds. Rusty twirled his hat until she grabbed it from him. He looked up at her with vacant eyes, as if to say, *so what?*

Andre stuck his hands in his pockets and turned to go. "You hungry?"

Rusty flashed a crooked smile. "Always." He leapt out of the chair and was at Andre's side in a second.

She fell in step with them and headed across the street to an Italian deli. She pulled Rusty into a booth while Andre went to retrieve some sandwiches.

"How long have you been on the streets?"

"About a year."

"Where are you from?"

"Different places. I tend to keep moving."

She noticed a paperback tucked into one of the coat pockets. "What are you reading?"

He withdrew a tattered copy of Henry David Thoreau's *Walden* and held it up for her inspection. She'd read it years ago during high school. The guy had stayed in a cabin, sacrificing most of his possessions to live simply. At the time she couldn't understand the message.

"Have you read it?" he asked.

"Years ago. I don't remember much."

He opened the book to a page he'd obviously studied thoroughly. It was a passage about simplicity and the frugal life. Two things were evident to her—he was a good reader and he understood the book. He definitely had one up on her. When he finished reading, he put it back in his pocket. "This is great stuff. It's what it's all about."

"What do you mean?"

"We have too many things in our life, too many responsibilities. We need to cut it down and focus only on the things that are important."

"You mean like family and education and friends?"

He seemed to bristle at her examples and turned to the window. He blinked quickly, and she thought she saw tears welling in his eyes. When he regained control, he faced her. "Education is the most important."

"Then why aren't you in school?"

"I am. This is my school." He gestured around the restaurant. "I've learned more in one year on the streets than I ever did in a classroom. I don't need to be there."

"But if you don't go to school, you'll never get off the streets. This way of learning will only get you so far."

He shrugged. "Maybe."

She could tell he was smarter than most of the street kids she'd met. He didn't automatically disagree with the truth. He saw it—he just wasn't ready to accept it yet, or he knew he needed school and didn't know how to go back. She dropped the conversation, recognizing there was nothing else to discuss. She'd learned from experience that questioning runaways meant leaving their pasts alone and avoiding lectures. She couldn't change the world, and they refused to answer questions about their families or backgrounds, which were usually shocking and horrific. She debated whether to haul him in, but she thought it would be pointless. He'd just run the first chance he had. She made a mental note to run a missing juvenile report to see if anyone was looking for him.

Andre arrived at the table and presented Rusty with two twelve-inch hoagies and a super-size drink. "Thanks, man," he offered. They watched Rusty slip one of the sandwiches into his pocket for later, and he wasted no time unrolling the paper and taking a huge bite. "Great."

"Rusty, we need to ask you about Itchy," Andre said.

He exhaled and shook his head. "So sad. That dude was okay. He really helped me a lot when I got to Phoenix. I think he felt sorry for me. Is it true that he's dead?" Rusty looked up at Andre, hoping the older man would tell him some good news. Molly saw the remnants of a regular kid in Rusty's eyes.

"Yeah, he's dead," Andre said. "And it wasn't pretty. Whoever did this to Itchy was trying to make a point."

Rusty continued to work his way through the sandwich, trying to be polite and not speak with his mouth full. "I heard he got stabbed and they left a note."

"Stabbed, shot and beheaded," Molly added. "This was a real hit, and Itchy paid a price for what he knew." She gently touched his arm. "And we're worried that Itchy might have told someone else."

Rusty shrugged. "I don't know anything. Itchy never talked about people being after him."

"We don't think he knew," Andre said. "He had some information, and either someone found out, or he tried to blackmail them and paid the price. If he told anybody, then that person could be in serious danger."

Rusty sipped his drink and seemed to contemplate Andre's words. Molly wasn't sure if he was deciding what to share with them or if he really didn't know Itchy's secrets. *Maybe,* Molly thought, *Rusty does know but he doesn't realize the importance of the information.* His gaze darted from Andre to Molly before returning to his lunch. "I can't help you."

"Can't or *won't,*" Molly said.

He swallowed the last bite and shook his head. "Doesn't matter. Same difference. I'm just a kid."

Molly stared at him. He did know something, but he wasn't sure he should tell. "That's right, Rusty, you are a kid, and as smart as you are, how long do you think you'll last on the streets without Itchy? You said he taught you a lot, and look what happened to him." Rusty's expression softened, and she was sure she'd struck a nerve. "You just need to tell us about your last conversation with Itchy. Let us decide what's important, and let us help you."

"We can make sure you get in a shelter or get some assistance," Andre added.

Rusty glared at him. "I don't need or *want* any help."

Andre held up a hand and nodded. "That's cool. It's just an offer. So when was the last time you saw Itchy?"

Rusty leaned against the cushion, as if he was settling in to tell a story. "I saw him about two weeks ago, on Monday and then Tuesday."

"Are you sure?" Molly asked.

"Yeah. Mondays are the day that this group serves snacks to the homeless in Patriot's Park, so we always used to see each other there. And Tuesday he came by the hotel while I was watching *CSI* on cable."

"What did he talk about that might be important to us? Did

120

he show you any money or did he talk about meeting anyone?"

Rusty cocked his head. "Geez, were you there? He brought me this huge takeout dinner, and when I asked him how he got it, he looked around to see if we were alone, and then he pulled this huge wad of cash from his pocket. It looked like a roll of twenties and fifties. I asked who died and he laughed. He said he was involved in a little business venture and this was his payoff. He said there was gonna be more soon and then he promised me that if he got enough money, he was gonna get off the streets, and he said I could come too. We'd get an apartment and be roommates." Rusty's head dropped to his chest. He took a deep breath before he looked up again. "He said I could go back to school. We ate and he left. Said he'd be in touch. That was the last time I saw him."

Molly let a few moments pass in silence. "What did he say about the business venture?"

"He said there was big money to be made. I asked him if I could get in on it, and he said no way. He wouldn't let me. He was kinda like that. Always looking out for me. He said he'd take care of me." Rusty paused and let the emotions wash over him. "He said he was going out on his own. He had a plan."

"To run drugs?" she asked skeptically.

"No, Itchy wouldn't get in that deep. He had a plan to strike it rich. I don't know what he was going to do, but he said it was a sure thing."

Andre pulled out a picture of the numbers written on the memo pad. "Have you ever seen this?"

Rusty peered at the photo and shook his head. "No."

"Did you ever see Itchy with any guys in suits? You know, guys who look like professionals?"

"No, but Itchy mentioned somebody named Ron or something—"

"Rondo?" Molly asked.

"Yeah, Rondo. Said he knew him. That's really all I know."

They talked with Rusty for another half hour, Andre guiding

much of the conversation about the Phoenix Suns, Rusty's favorite team. He saw the games regularly, depending on a friendly security guard to slip him through an underground garage door. As she often did, Molly distanced herself from the conversation, partly because of her aversion to small talk, but also because she wanted to study Rusty. While her heart ached for any juvenile stuck on the street, there was a savvy about him, a streetwise common sense that usually took years to develop. She felt two conflicting emotions at once, empathy and caution. She couldn't be sure if he was telling her the whole truth. Streetwise kids could also be exceptional liars.

They dropped him off in front of the apartment building and drove back to One Police Plaza while they processed the conversation and Rusty's relationship with Itchy.

"Based on what Rusty told us, I don't understand why Itchy had the drugs," she said. "Rusty said Itchy wouldn't do that, but he was caught with them, and different witnesses saw him with a wad of cash. How else would he make that money?" She glanced at Andre, who had no answer. "When I interrogated him after we found the drugs, he said it was a one-time thing, and I believed him."

"Mol, you can't beat yourself up. He'd never given you reason to doubt him. His info always checked out. I believed him, too. It's really out of character for him. Itchy was low-level. Fencing stolen property was his game. I wonder what changed."

"He'd had enough of the street life."

"You know, the cash might be about the numbers."

"How?"

Andre shrugged. "I don't know, but getting involved with Rondo was definitely moving into the big leagues—fast."

Molly shook her head. She prided herself on understanding human motivation and following her gut feelings, and now it was telling her this wasn't right. She turned to Andre. "You up for doing some research or do you have a hot date?"

Andre grinned seductively. "No, I'm saving myself for Ari's

party. I'll find me a fine woman there."

At the mention of Ari, Molly frowned. She hadn't decided what to do. She was terrible at fighting and she tended to retreat afterward. Whether it was her pride or her ignorance, Ari had to take her hand and walk her through the steps of reconciliation. It didn't matter who started the fight or what it was about. Molly was truly incapable of bringing them back together, and since Ari had not initiated contact since their horrible phone call the day before, she doubted Ari wanted to see her, and she didn't want to go home to an empty apartment.

She pulled her lips into a grudging smile. "I'm positive you're going to lose this bet. So does that mean you got the time to work?"

"Yeah. Let's go back and dig up some dirt on our new best friend John Rondo."

Chapter Twenty

Tuesday, October 17th
4:18 PM

Ari learned more information about Aspen through her search on the Internet. Aspen's journey west to Phoenix from a little town in New York was dotted with many stops along the way, each city a little larger and each opportunity more prestigious. Ari was surprised at the number of restaurant reviews that mentioned Aspen as the chef, and all were complimentary, exclaiming her talent and praising the establishment for hiring such a culinary wonder. She clearly didn't shy away from the spotlight, and Ari opened several picture files featuring Aspen in her white chef coat with various local power brokers, including the mayor of Milwaukee, the governor of Missouri and several celebrities. Over the years her appearance had changed slightly as she grew her strawberry blond hair out to its current shoulder length, but her face remained youthful and attractive. When she strung together the pieces of Aspen's bio, it portrayed a woman on the rise looking for advancement and prestige at every turn.

She skimmed the last review in the *Albuquerque Journal*, another gushing testimonial to Aspen's talents. It wasn't until she reached the last few lines that a sentence caught her eye. *If Ms. Harper can manage to stay out of the gossip column and concentrate fully on her craft, she will undoubtedly become one of the greatest chefs this city has ever known.*

Her eyes narrowed and she checked the date—April twenty-fifth of the previous year. Obviously something juicy had happened that would cause the reviewer to mention it. She scrolled to the top of the column and found the writer's name, Courtney Belmont. A few more clicks of the mouse and she located the newspaper's main line.

"Thank God for technology," she said, dialing the number.

"*Albuquerque Journal*," a pleasant voice said.

"Hello, I'm looking for Courtney Belmont, your restaurant critic."

"Let me check my directory. I'm not familiar with that name." Ari listened as the woman tapped on her computer keyboard a few hundred miles away. "Huh. I'm not seeing a listing for a Courtney Belmont at this paper. Let me transfer you to the home and living editor who oversees our food section."

Before she could thank the operator, another two clicks sounded in her ear and a young, nervous voice answered. "Home and living section. This is Mary speaking."

"Hi. I'm calling from Phoenix, and I read a review by one of your reporters, a Courtney Belmont? I was hoping to speak with her."

"Um, she doesn't work here anymore. Is there some way I can help you?"

"Is this the editor of the home section?"

"Uh, no. That's Mr. McMahon. He's in a meeting right now. Would you like to call back? I could take a message."

Mary sounded as though she really wanted Ari to leave a message. Ari smiled. Mary was exactly the kind of person who might divulge more information than she should. "Actually, Mary, you might be able to help me. You said Courtney Belmont didn't work there anymore. When did she quit?"

"About eight months ago."

"Did she say where she was going?"

"Um, well . . ."

Ari could hear the hesitation in Mary's voice. She was most likely a good Girl Scout who was smart enough to distrust strangers. "Look, Mary, here's the thing. I know you don't know me, but I'm a friend of Courtney's from high school, and we lost touch a while back. I Googled her and found this review she wrote, and that's why I called you guys. I really need to find her. Her grandmother is dying, and she wants to see Courtney before she goes." Ari cringed at the lie, but the image of Jane's destroyed bedroom quickly balanced her conscience.

"Oh, that's very sad. I know what it's like to lose your grandma."

"I'm sorry. Did your grandmother pass?"

"Not like that. She got lost in Wal-Mart last week. Her mind is really going."

Ari shook her head and rolled her eyes. "So, getting back to Courtney, do you know why she quit?"

"Uh, I can't really be sure," Mary replied. "I didn't know her very well. She wasn't one of our regular reporters. We contracted with her to do food reviews, so she just popped in once every couple of weeks. We barely said more than a few words."

"Do you know where she went?"

"L.A., I think."

Ari scribbled notes and paused. "Mary, I was reading this review by Courtney, and it was about Aspen Harper, the chef. She sounded intriguing. What's the story on her?"

"She was this great chef, but she got herself into a real mess." Mary's voice grew animated, and Ari could tell she wanted to share the gossip.

"What happened?"

"Well," Mary began, lowering her voice, "an angry customer at the Haven, that's the name of the restaurant where she worked, made a scene one night and demanded to see her. He was some bigwig financial asshole who thought he could push people around. Aspen came out to talk to him and his girlfriend, and in front of the entire restaurant he screams at her that the soup was cold, and the salmon was dry—whatever. I never really heard all of the details. Anyway, the story goes that she stood there quietly and listened. Never said a word. Just took it until he was done and then walked back into her kitchen."

"Sounds like she handled it appropriately," Ari said. "Why would that be a problem?"

"It wouldn't if that's where the story ended. So the girlfriend is this high-profile attorney, and by the next week, her picture is in the local gossip rag, and she's kissing another woman outside of this lesbian bar, and guess who the woman is?"

"Aspen Harper."

"You got it. The paparazzi, or what little of it there is in Albuquerque, went crazy. And then two days later, the police get a call from the guy that his Mercedes has been vandalized. Somebody poured acid all over his hood."

"Wow. How did they connect that to Aspen?"

"Well, they didn't really. Courtney did. She'd just done a profile on Aspen Harper and thought the woman was a little off. After all this happened she went back to the restaurant and confronted Aspen. She thought there might be a story."

"And was there?"

"You know, that's the weird part. She'd been all gung-ho about going after Aspen, and then she totally flipped. She never talked to me, just Dennis, the editor. I overheard her arguing with him one day, saying that she was wrong and that there really wasn't anything there. Dennis wanted her to dig a lot more, but she wanted to drop it, and she did. He was pretty furious. She quit soon after that."

"So Aspen never went to court for vandalizing the Mercedes?"

"Nope. The guy collected on the insurance and I'll bet he never ate at the Haven again." Mary laughed.

"So was there any other press on Aspen?"

Ari heard Mary exhale. "No, Aspen left Albuquerque around that time. Come to think of it, she went to Phoenix, didn't she?"

"Yes, she's working as a chef at an upscale restaurant."

"Well, just make sure you never criticize her cooking. Word to the wise."

"So Courtney's in L.A. now?"

"I think so, but who knows?"

Ari's radar pricked up and she stopped doodling on her pad. "Why do you say that?"

"She didn't give any notice. She just showed up one morning with a memo saying that she was severing her ties with the *Journal* and her last check could be forwarded to someplace in L.A. I was walking by when she left Dennis's office and we chatted for a minute."

"What did she say?"

"Not much. I asked her lots of questions about where she was going, and why she was leaving, but she was evasive. It wouldn't surprise me if she never went to L.A." Mary paused, and Ari could tell she was trying to remember something. "There was one interesting point."

"What was that?"

"She'd bought a new car. I followed her out to the front of the building and said good-bye, and when I looked out the window, I saw her get into a red Dodge Viper."

"What?" Ari's hand froze in midsentence. "Are you sure?"

"Yeah, I'm sure. And I laughed, wondering how she would ever afford it. Anyway, that's all I know. I've gotta go. I'm only an intern and I need to keep working."

Ari thanked her and hung up the phone. She leaned back in her chair and stared at the final note she'd added: *Courtney Belmont & Aspen Harper = red Dodge Viper.*

Chapter Twenty-one
Tuesday, October 17ᵗʰ
7:47 PM

Ari glanced at her watch and sat up on Molly's couch. She knew if she remained horizontal for much longer she would fall into a deep sleep. Molly still wasn't home, and a pang of sympathy hit her. Molly was working so hard on this case, trying to rise within the ranks of the police department. She smiled at the thought, certain that Molly would succeed, and she had seen firsthand how capable and competent Molly was at her job.

She went to the kitchen and stirred the pot of stew that waited on the stove. At least when Molly arrived, a wonderful smell would greet her, and she hoped that her peace offering would be enough to dissolve the detective's jealousy over her bizarre luncheon with Biz Stone. Thinking about Biz was something she tried to avoid. She knew her feelings were more conflicted than she wanted to admit, but she believed what she told Jane. She could be fascinated by a woman and not physically involved. She nodded her head in agreement and kept stirring. Engaged in the mundane task, her mind drifted to the phone call she'd made to Biz a few hours ago, eager to share the new information about Aspen Harper.

Biz agreed to check out Courtney Belmont, and she told Ari that Isabel Collins was a complicated lady who had a restraining order against her from a few years back—for stalking a woman. Ari could imagine either Aspen or Isabel leaving the flowers, and while their investigation seemed focused on those two leads, the fact was, the list of suspects was endless. Jane's sexual antics could have ignited the fuse of several hotheaded women, and when Ari remembered some of the screaming matches that occurred in the Hideaway bathroom, she knew Jane was frequently the reason.

The lock on the apartment door clicked and Molly glanced instantly toward the kitchen. Ari offered a slight smile but stayed behind the counter while Molly remained just inside the closed door. It occurred to her that they'd advanced into unknown territory. Their past arguments were trivial compared to this one. They had never fought over another woman.

"I heard about last night," Molly said. "Is Jane okay?"

"Yeah. She's staying with me for now."

Molly nodded and studied the floor. "I'm sorry I didn't call you back. I guess that's why you kept calling me, huh?" Her gaze flicked up and quickly darted back to the carpet.

"Well, that and the fact that I nearly threw up after our phone conversation."

Molly shifted her feet, still unable to look at her. "I said some horrible things. I can't even imagine why you're here."

"Did you mean what you said? Do you really believe we have no commitment to each other?"

Molly looked up with tears in her eyes. "Of course I didn't mean it. I was just so jealous."

"Don't be. I don't want to talk about this anymore, okay? Biz is a business associate, and if you and I are going to have a relationship, then you need to trust me. Do you trust me?"

Molly looked at Ari as though the thought never occurred to her. "Of course I trust you."

Ari smiled seductively. "So, detective, what are you doing way over there?"

Molly flew into her arms and their bodies clung to each other as if they'd been apart for months. She held her, and she felt Molly's body heave with sobs.

"It's all right, honey. It's okay."

"I'm just so sorry."

She reached for a towel and wiped Molly's cheeks. "I know." Their lips connected, igniting the passion that always seemed to smolder just below the surface. Molly pushed her against the refrigerator and unsnapped her jeans.

"Can dinner wait?" Molly whispered.

"That's why I made stew. It can simmer for a while."

Molly grinned and pulled her out of the kitchen and into the bedroom for an hour. At one point, Ari jumped out of bed to stir the stew, and when she returned, Molly had lit some candles and turned on some jazz.

"I take it we're not finished here?" Ari said.

Molly pulled her naked body against her own and they slid into bed again. "No," she said simply.

Ari leaned back and closed her eyes while Molly's lips traveled across her body, kissing her everywhere. Her hips found a pleasant rhythm, and when Molly's long fingers went deep inside her, she cried out in ecstasy, but Molly wouldn't let go—not until she came twice more. They lay together, and then, as was her ritual, Molly left her and went to the living room and the piano. Ari closed her eyes, listening to the composition Molly was creating, a tribute to her—to their love. Eventually she joined her on the bench, watching her fingers fly across the ivory keys, her face molded into a different kind of passion. She loved watching her compose music. Since she wrote nothing down, she played up to a point, and then she began experimenting, and Ari loved listening to the amazing results. Molly would play several different measures of music, and Ari was always curious to see which one she picked, which blend of notes would be attached to the score. Suddenly Molly stopped playing and reached for her. She kissed her and pushed her down on the piano bench.

"You are insatiable," Ari said.

Molly grinned. "I know, but the smell of that stew is driving me crazy. I need some nourishment."

"Then we'd better eat—food," Ari added with a laugh.

They threw on some clothes and ate at Molly's breakfast bar, chatting about the day, avoiding the subject of Jane's orchids, which Ari realized would bring them back to Biz.

"You haven't forgotten about my party on Friday, have you?"

Molly cracked a smile and stirred her stew. "Not a chance."

"Did you get me a present?"

"Not yet, but I do have some gift ideas. I'm thinking either a circular saw or a man-hating voodoo doll."

Ari laughed. "God, someone needs to help my father understand lesbians."

"Well, I think understanding his own daughter would be a start. I guess for some parents, it's just not easy to deal with their children. I never had that problem. My family was always so close, and I assumed it was that way for everyone else."

"You were lucky. Your family skipped a lot of tragedy. I'm sure there were rough times, but they weren't insurmountable."

Molly looked at her seriously and touched her cheek. "I know your life was much different. I know how lucky I was as a kid and how lucky I am now to have you."

The weight of Molly's words hit her. Years before, at a much different time, she hadn't been so sure she wanted to live. Now, she couldn't imagine wanting to end her life. She kissed Molly's hand and stared into her crystal blue eyes. "So how was your day?"

Molly shared her concerns about Rusty. "That boy is too wise for his own good," she concluded.

"Are you sure he told you everything he knows?"

Molly glanced at her. "There are times, baby, when I really think you should have stayed on the police force. Your instincts are always so good." She finished off her stew, leaned back and caressed Ari's arm. "No, I'm not totally convinced. There's something about him that makes me second-guess what he said. He did confirm that Itchy was working for a guy named John Rondo."

Ari turned to her. "Why does that name sound familiar?"

"He's been mentioned a few times on the news because he's mafia. He's a relative of the Carnotti family."

That name Ari knew well. "That was Dad's case several years ago."

Molly rested her chin on her hand, clearly interested. "What do you remember about it?"

"Well, it started as a drug bust gone bad. An undercover cop wound up dead, and my father was the lead detective on the case. They eventually got a conviction of a cousin of Carnotti, but they could never tie the trail directly back to him. I remember something about evidence disappearing, too."

Molly arched her eyebrows. "Really? What happened with that?"

"Nothing. Dad could never prove it, but he was rather sure someone was on the take." She felt a knot forming in her throat. "I think he dropped it because it was around the time that I came out and my mom got sick again."

"Oh," Molly said. "I can see why. We don't have to talk about it anymore. That was a long time ago."

"Do you think it could have anything to do with your case now?"

"Highly unlikely. Most of those guys have all retired, and none of the players are the same. Now, no more talk about work. I keep getting this image of David Ruskin in my head, standing over my desk and yelling at me." Molly pecked her on the cheek and began carrying dishes into the kitchen.

Ari instantly smirked at the mention of Ruskin, a man she detested and who had sexually harassed her whenever she'd visited her father at the precinct. "You definitely don't need him in your head." She drained her wineglass and joined Molly. "I'm sure that he thinks this could somehow advance his career."

"Of course. He's the talking head for the department."

"Lucky you. Still, you get to work with the FBI, so it could help your career, too."

"Hopefully," Molly said. "I'll say one thing, from what Connie Rasp has told me, working for the FBI isn't much different than the Phoenix P.D., at least if you're gay."

"Oh, I didn't realize she was gay." Ari glanced at Molly before she added, "Is she attractive?"

Within seconds Molly was blushing, and she wouldn't look up from the sink. She shrugged, but her face had already betrayed her. "I guess so."

Ari grinned and rested her chin on Molly's shoulder, trying hard not to laugh. "How attractive would you say she is?" Molly stammered for an answer and her face grew redder while Ari's grin widened. "Really hot, huh?"

"Baby, it's strictly professional," Molly said defensively.

Ari cupped Molly's chin in her hand. "I know it is. And I trust you, too."

Molly nodded in understanding and kissed her. They cleaned up the kitchen, and Ari mused over their simple domesticity. They fell into their unspoken assigned roles, Molly stacking the dishwasher while she cleaned the counters and scoured the stewpot. She knew she could spend every night like this with Molly, but she kept her thoughts to herself. She watched the sink drain and wiped her hands on a towel.

Molly's strong arms encircled her waist, and she nibbled on her ear. "Are you staying the night or do you need to get home to Jane?"

She laughed. "Jane's not home. She's out at Hideaway, and I'm rather sure she'll be spending the night in someone else's bed. It's just a theory, but I'd bet my next commission on it. Sex is Jane's way of forgetting her troubles."

Molly kissed her neck, and she leaned back into the embrace. "Well, I think you should stay here tonight. We could curl up in bed and watch a movie."

"Hmm," Ari said, her eyes closed. "What movie did you have in mind?"

"I thought of *White Oleander*."

Ari laughed. "Or we could watch *Flower Drum Song*."

"What about *Flowers for Algernon*?"

Ari thought for a second before she said, "*Driving Miss Daisy*?"

They both laughed and retreated to the bedroom, their sanctuary from work.

Chapter Twenty-two
Tuesday, October 17th
11:54 PM

Hideaway's dance floor couldn't accommodate the swell of lesbians grinding and twisting to the music bursting from the oversize speakers. Women moved freely between partners, a few danced with groups, and some, like Jane, set their sights on a woman who danced alone. Jane shimmied against a voluptuous femme, her hands roaming down the woman's sizable hips.

From her stool at the opposite side of the bar, she watched. She avoided eye contact with everyone and chose to sit in the shadows of the bar. She projected herself as observer, not participant. She'd been there two hours and not a single woman had asked her to dance, which was fine. She was there to watch Jane. Occasionally she glanced at the dance floor and Jane's progress with the femme. They were leaning against each other, thrusting their hips together, as if starting a fire between them. The femme reached up and unbuttoned Jane's shirt, exposing much of her cleavage.

Jane stepped away to give her the show she wanted. She danced alone while the femme, and many of the other dancers, watched her shameless exhibitionism. She reached behind her head and thrust her chest forward. It was obvious she was braless, as her breasts gently bounced to the music. She was an exceptional dancer, her gyrations revealing enough to be risqué but not indecent.

She thought Jane was truly magnificent, and she couldn't tear her eyes away. The femme remained rooted in one place until Jane brushed past her and took her hand. They ducked into the back room, and the crowd resumed their own displays of sexuality on the dance floor.

She finished her martini and moved toward the door where Jane had disappeared. Two women emerged, locked in an embrace. She imagined they would head straight for the exit and the nearest motel—if they could wait that long.

She slipped into the darkness of the back room. Soft jazz muffled the quiet conversations and hushed whispers of the women who lounged on the plush couches, limbs and torsos splayed across them. She thought they looked like mannequins tossed aside, but the silhouettes moved together, kissing, touching and innocently fondling. It was the complete picture of foreplay— the legal part of sex. Everyone was clothed, and a few provincial couples sat a foot apart, holding hands and talking quietly. Only a few lamps glowed, providing enough light for players to identify their partners and connect with the desired body parts. While the rules of the back room explicitly forbade sexual touching, who would know if a thumb innocently grazed a nipple?

Most of the patrons clearly stayed on the side of decency— except Jane. She caught sight of the femme's bleach-blond hair as it rose above the back of a couch off to the left. She moved slowly in that direction, her eyes focused on the couch—where she knew Jane lay—when she unexpectedly felt arms wrap around her middle. Strong hands groped her breasts, and lips kissed her neck.

"Who are you watching?" the stranger asked.

"No one," she lied.

"Is it the brunette over there?"

She saw the brunette—her head thrown back over the arm of a couch while her partner kissed her neck. "No," she said.

"Then who?"

The stranger's hands slid inside her waistband and caressed her belly. Her eyes remained focused on Jane's couch, but she sighed when the stranger's fingers burrowed inside her bikini briefs. Suddenly Jane shot up from the couch and kissed the femme deeply.

"It's her, isn't it?" the stranger asked.

"Yes," she admitted.

"Do you love her?"

"I do. She's the only one for me."

"But she's with someone else."

She parted her legs slightly, and the stranger's fingers swept across her crotch. She sighed as she explained, "She doesn't know she wants me—yet."

"She won't want you. She's not the type to want anyone."

Her temper rose, and she tried to pull away, but the stranger held her tightly.

"Look at her," the stranger continued. "You can tell she enjoys sex. She could never be monogamous."

Tears rolled down her cheeks. The stranger was right. Jane was a whore, and she needed to be taught a lesson. Jane needed to change, and she realized how she could help. She would take what Jane valued most.

"Here's a proposition," the stranger whispered. "I'll fuck you and you pretend that you're fucking her."

She grabbed the stranger's busy hand and exited the back room, heading for her car and privacy.

Chapter Twenty-three

Wednesday, October 18ᵗʰ

8:18 AM

Files and printouts stretched across Molly's desk, a paper trail of John Rondo's professional and personal life. Andre had minored in finance during college, so he analyzed the business holdings of Johnson Enterprises, which was really just an umbrella company owned by Rondo using his wife's maiden name. Molly learned what she could about the man through his credit cards. Much of the shopping was done by his wife, Jennifer, a respectable Yale graduate with a business degree. An Internet article showed the Rondos at a charity function, their cute children in tow. Molly shook her head when she saw that each month he still amassed hundreds of dollars of charges at the High Life, Phoenix's premier gentlemen's club, despite being married to an incredibly beautiful and intelligent woman who had her own Web site and designed upscale purses.

"What are you finding?" Andre asked across the sea of paper.

Molly leaned back and stretched. "Guy's got a gorgeous wife, who's more than a trophy, but he's still hitting the clubs, and she spends an easy three grand at Saks Fifth Avenue in an afternoon."

Andre snorted and dropped a file on the desk. "Then I guess they both get what they want. And they've got it to spend. Rondo's easily worth five mil, and that's the money I *can* find. God only knows how much he's hidden, and how many dummy corporations he's created to launder Carnotti's money."

Molly picked up the phone. "Let's call Rasp and see if the fibbies have better luck. Maybe their data banks can give us an accurate profile of John Rondo. While they're looking, we can go visit the man." When the call immediately went to voice mail, she left a quick message for Rasp to call her, and she and Andre headed for the car.

They had reached the lobby when Sol Gardener and David Ruskin came around the corner. Sol smiled and Ruskin immediately frowned and stuck his hands into his pockets.

"Molly, how good to see you," Sol said, squeezing her arm. "David tells me that your informant was murdered."

I'm sure he did, she thought. "Yeah, he was hit and left in a trunk. We're working on a new lead, the guy who owned the building where the meet was supposed to happen. Have you heard of John Rondo?"

Sol searched his memory and slowly nodded his head. "Yes." He turned and pointed at Ruskin. "Wasn't he involved somehow in that case with Jack Adams?"

Ruskin only shrugged. Molly smiled slightly at his clear discomfort. He hated Ari's father, the man who had hazed him endlessly during his rookie year in an effort to push him to quit.

"For some reason," Sol continued, "I thought he was connected. Maybe you should call Jack."

Molly froze, unable to fathom how she would ever have a conversation with Ari's father when he had no idea she was his daughter's lover. She only nodded and waved good-bye as they hurried away to the elevator.

Andre covered his mouth, but he couldn't silence his chuckle. "Yes, why don't you call Jack? You could introduce yourself."

Molly ignored him and breezed through the door into the parking lot. They grappled with the last few minutes of morning rush-hour traffic and headed toward central Phoenix and the Biltmore Corridor, the most expensive commercial real estate in Phoenix. Rondo's offices were located in the Esplanade, a matching set of glass twin towers that boasted extraordinary views of Camelback Mountain. They pulled into the visitor parking and took the elevator to the lobby. From there Molly could see Rondo's personal digs—a multimillion-dollar condo building called the Embers that hugged the Esplanade property. The homes stretched to the sky, and she knew the cheapest ones were valued at two million.

"I wonder if he walks to work," Andre mused.

"I doubt it," Molly replied. "He probably *still* takes his Mercedes, just to use his private parking space."

They rode up to the twentieth floor and saw that Johnson Enterprises and Rondo Dynamics filled the entire floor with several offices. As Andre checked in with the receptionist, Molly toured the lobby, noting the expensive furniture and several hallways with offices and cubicles, but after ten minutes, she only saw three employees and never heard the phone ring.

"You'd think it was a holiday," she whispered to Andre.

"It is. It's Bust Your Favorite Money Launderer Day."

"Now, Andre, we shouldn't be too quick to judge."

Andre rifled through a back copy of *Phoenix Living*. "Right."

After five more minutes of waiting, she returned to the receptionist with a scowl on her face. "We need to see John Rondo right now, or we'll go look for him ourselves."

Clearly that idea seemed far less desirable to the twig-like blonde, who used her pencil to punch in numbers on the enormous phone bank. She whispered into the headset, and Molly was sure the young girl really had no idea what occurred at Rondo Dynamics, which was probably a good thing. Molly turned away and stared down the corridor. A man in a blue suit turned the corner, and she instantly recognized him as John Rondo. He looked like a large football player with a buzz cut, and from the way he walked, she guessed he hated wearing a suit. It clung to him as if it were still on the hanger.

"Detectives," he said, shaking their hands, "I'm John Rondo. Let's go to my office." They followed him down the long corridor, past several closed doors to another waiting area without a receptionist. Molly noted the soft lighting and the smell of expensive leather, a marked difference from the reception area.

"Your assistant has the day off?" Andre asked, pointing to the vacant desk, which Molly noticed was devoid of any personal belongings.

"We're in the middle of a restructuring. Several employees have been let go or been reassigned."

She let the lame explanation go without comment. Rondo led them into a spacious corner office with glass on two sides. He had an incredible view of Camelback Mountain, Piestewa Peak and much of the Central Corridor high-rises in between. The office befitted the CEO of a large company, complete with reading area and wet bar. The walls were covered with B-movie posters, mostly alien thrillers depicting large-breasted women holding some sort of weapon. To Molly, they equated to photos usually found on garage calendars, but because they were cartoons, they seemed less offensive. She imagined that Rondo and many of his goons enjoyed staring at the scantily clad caricatures. Behind his desk was a credenza full of framed photos of him with his wife and two sons, creating a balance between skirt-chaser and family man. He motioned for them to sit and dropped his large frame into an expensive executive chair.

"How can I help you?"

She and Andre had worked a strategy in the car, one that required her to let him lead the conversation. She hated being in

142

the second chair, but she'd been a cop long enough to recognize that macho men responded better to other men.

Andre glanced at his notepad and cleared his throat. "Okay, let's start with the basics. Do you know a man named Dudley Moon? On the street he goes by Itchy."

Rondo shook his head. "Never heard of him."

"So you wouldn't have any idea how his body and severed head wound up in a trunk at the airport?"

Rondo held up his huge hands and Molly noticed he wore no rings, not even a wedding band. His wrist, however, sported an extremely expensive watch. "Look, detectives, I'm a business-man. Despite what the feds think, I don't get involved with my family. Yeah, Vinnie's my cousin, and every year we exchange Christmas presents, and we see each other once or twice. He's family, but I don't know anything about his business."

It was a well-rehearsed speech, one that Molly imagined he'd delivered to the FBI and the Justice Department. "So are you suggesting that Vince Carnotti had something to do with the execution of Dudley Moon?"

Rondo paled, recognizing his mistake. "I'm not suggesting it. You are. Why else would you be here?"

"Maybe because we're interested in Rondo Dynamics," Andre said. "Maybe we'd like to learn more about your company. What exactly do you do here, Mr. Rondo?"

He shifted in his seat and smiled pleasantly at Andre's ques-tion. "Rondo Dynamics and the Johnson Corporation are largely middlemen who deal in the buying and selling of medical equip-ment and parts."

Molly recognized the advantage of Rondo's role: much money and goods traded hands, and if anything was laundered along the way, it would be very difficult to prove. It was the perfect cover. "What can you tell us about Cactus Airpark?" she asked, unable to keep silent any longer. "We were told that a drug buy might be occurring, and when we went out there, the entire place was abandoned. It looked like someone tipped them off. Do you know anything about that?"

Her sarcasm wasn't lost on Rondo, who smiled easily. It was obvious they couldn't prove anything, and he showed no sign of discomfort. "I assure you there wasn't any drug buy happening on that property. Right now Cactus Airpark is undergoing a major renovation. Many of our tenants have found other arrangements in the meantime. I'm sure that's what you saw."

"Of course," Andre answered.

Molly tapped Andre on the arm with the back of her hand. "I'll bet the construction crews are on their way over there right now to knock out a few walls and install some new plumbing."

Rondo chuckled. "I assure you that I have all of the proper paperwork for the project. Would you like to see the plans?" He grabbed a roll of drawings from behind him and dropped them onto his desk with great ceremony.

Andre leaned forward. "I just want to make sure I'm clear, in case we have to have another conversation downtown at some point. You don't know anything about the murder of Itchy Moon."

Rondo shook his head. "No, I wish I could help you, but I don't make it a habit to associate with street people."

"Does that include prostitutes?" Molly asked pointedly.

Rondo glared at her. "Detective, in case you haven't noticed, I am a happily married man." They glanced at the photos displayed on Rondo's credenza, all of them depicting two beautiful children with angelic smiles, their arms wrapped around Rondo and his wife, a buxom beauty. Molly was certain her oversized chest was financed by Rondo's money-laundering deals.

"Half of the men in America are married and have visited a prostitute," she said. "Having a family doesn't exempt you. We do know you've spent quite a bit more time and money at the High Life than most married men."

Rondo didn't answer, but she knew she'd hit a nerve, and the façade crumbled. "Detectives, I think it's time you left. I have nothing else to say." He strolled to the office door and opened it, waiting for them to exit.

She could feel Rondo's eyes on her back as she went down the hallway. The man was too smart to slam his door shut in a huff, leaving them to accidentally veer down the wrong corridor and deeper into the heart of Rondo Dynamics. It wasn't until they were within sight of the receptionist that Molly heard the door close.

"That guy is so transparent," Andre said when they got in their car. "Do you think he killed Itchy?"

"Oh, he's definitely involved."

She could feel the acid in her stomach starting to churn. There was something bothering her, something she knew she should remember from their meeting with Rondo, and she was missing it. She pulled her notebook from her jacket pocket and drew a circle. She put Itchy at the center and drew circles around him. She included Rondo, Carnotti and Rusty. The she added one more and put a question mark in the middle. Her stomachache flared at the thought of a fellow officer on the take. Yet it was too coincidental. She thought of Jack Adams and his hunches. He was highly respected, and Carnotti must have sighed in relief when Jack stepped away from his suspicions. She pulled her cell phone out and punched in the numbers for Sol Gardener's secretary. It clicked immediately to voice mail, and Molly found herself relieved.

"Hey, Mona, it's Molly Nelson. Can you call me back on my cell? I need the number for Jack Adams."

Chapter Twenty-four
Wednesday, October 18th
1:45 PM

Ari's morning was an enjoyable whirlwind of activity. As a real estate agent, the best part of her job was a closing, a moment when she got to present a buyer with the keys to his new house or a seller with the good news that the deal was sealed and a check was waiting. Either way meant a payday for her and today she closed two transactions, a rare but lucrative event. Of course, one of the deals had stalled in escrow over bureaucratic paperwork by an incompetent title officer, and she should have been paid two weeks before. But she always welcomed a commission—even if it was late. And two in the same day was a great boost for the ego, particularly in a slumping economy.

It was after one o'clock when she finally returned to Southwest Realty after traversing the valley to attend meetings at the different title companies. As she checked her phone messages, a figure

146

crossed the yard pushing a wheelbarrow full of bricks. At first she thought it was Gilberto, the man who gardened for Lorraine, but she realized it was a woman—Jane's handy-dyke, Teri. She watched Teri stack the bricks into neat piles and cordon off a section of the yard for a planter. Curious, Ari cradled the phone and went out back.

Teri looked up and grinned. "Hey, Ari."

"Hi, Teri. It's great to see you, but don't you have enough to do working on Jane's investment?"

Teri wiped her hands on her jeans. "You can't tell Jane I'm here. She would have a fit if she knew I was still doing odd jobs on the side. The fact is, I need the money and I can't do anything else on the house today. I have the time, but Jane would never understand. Can you keep my secret?"

"Sure." Ari noticed a planter design sketched haphazardly on a piece of paper, which Teri had pinned to the wooden fence. "I didn't realize you knew Lorraine or that you did landscaping. Your talent is really amazing."

Teri blushed and kicked her boot against the grass. "Thanks. I met Lorraine a few years ago when she hired me to remodel this place. I've done construction practically my entire life, since I got out of high school. I just like the idea of creating the whole picture, you know. I have these plans for my dream house, and I've designed every detail—inside and out."

Ari could hear the pride in Teri's voice. She also longed for a home and was tired of living in a condo. Yet she had no idea what she would want, and she hadn't taken any steps to change her life. Her relationship with Molly was probably a factor, but she didn't want to analyze it. She pointed to the bricks. "So what will go in these planters?"

"I haven't decided yet. Because of the exposure, I won't plant anything that can't withstand the heat. The sun's going to shine directly on this area for most of the day, so we don't want flowers here that are really fragile. They'll die in a week."

At the mention of flowers, Ari's ears pricked up. "Do you

147

know a lot about flowers?"

Teri shrugged. "I'm not a horticulturist, but I've studied on my own."

"Do you have a garden at your place?"

"No, I live in an apartment, so I have to get my fix working for other people." Teri glanced at her watch and grabbed her pick. "And I need to get started if I'm going to be back at Jane's investment before she comes by."

Ari stepped away. "I won't keep you. See you, Teri."

"Hey, Ari, how is Jane doing? I heard about what happened."

"She's holding up. I think she's more upset than she wants anyone to believe."

"So she's staying with you?" Teri's voice quivered as she asked the question, as though she were disappointed.

"Yeah, I gave her my spare bedroom. She never wants to go back to her condo."

Teri nodded and dropped the pick into the lawn. "I guess that's understandable."

Ari watched as she ripped a line in the ground, focused on her work. Ari returned to her office and settled into her chair. Her gaze wandered out to Teri, who had found her rhythm with the pick, now an extension of her muscled arms. Ari couldn't help herself. Watching Teri was like watching a living sculpture. Her body was flawless. She blinked and shook her head. *Why was she having these thoughts?* She replayed the exchange from the beginning, when she saw Teri through the window and walked outside. She'd glanced at the bricks, Teri had spoken with her and she'd seen the sketch—and the stationery with the yellow marigold emblem from Cavanaugh Flowers.

Ari wheeled back around to her computer and pulled up the Cavanaugh Flowers Web site. She scrolled through the home page, learning that the company was the oldest flower shop in Surprise. The Webmaster had included some photos of Mr. and Mrs. Cavanaugh, as well as a few of the shop. She didn't know what she expected to find, but she read every word carefully

148

and clicked through all of the links, learning that orchids were indeed very expensive, and she would never pay the price for an elephant orchid. She clicked back to the home page and glanced through her window. She could just go ask Teri if she worked for Cavanaugh Flowers, but if Teri was Jane's stalker, she wasn't sure how wise that would be, confronting a crazy woman with a pick. She let out a deep breath. Could Teri really be the stalker? She'd known Jane for a while and seemed to have little interest in her romantically. From what Jane had said Teri had rejected *her*, which wouldn't give her much motive. Yet Ari's conversation with Teri in the yard was weird. She sensed there was energy between Teri and Jane that she couldn't place. Perhaps it was just Teri's concern—or perhaps it was more. She scrolled through the thumbnails on the Cavanaugh Flowers home page once more, and one photo caught her attention. It was an exterior shot of the greenhouse. At the edge of the picture was the corner of a truck. She enlarged the photo and confirmed her suspicions. The photographer had accidentally included the tailgate of a rusty, banana-yellow Dodge pickup that looked exactly like Teri's truck.

Chapter Twenty-five
Wednesday, October 18th
6:48 PM

As was her custom, Molly saved her paperwork for Wednesday nights, the middle of the week, when she knew she could stay as late as she needed. It was her night away from Ari, and while she would have much preferred to be in Ari's arms, she took a sense of comfort in having the time alone in the building, when she could work in peace and look out on the streets from her fourth-story window. Downtown was busy tonight, and cars streamed toward the parking garages and the Phoenix Suns' game. She watched the headlights, glowing white eyes slithering along, energizing the downtown's nightlife.

She glanced at the file on her desk—Itchy's file—and the gruesome pictures of his body. She flipped through the M.E.'s report again, focusing on the bruise under his eye. Dr. Haynes had confirmed that the indentation was most likely that of a ring with a significant stone. Rondo had worn no jewelry, but that didn't mean anything. She would need to check around and see if people usually saw him wearing a ring. Judging by the size of his hands, any ring that fit his finger would be huge. He was definitely the prime suspect, only because there was no one else. She realized that the actual doer could have been most anyone on Carnotti's payroll, but she liked John Rondo, and his connection to the original meeting place Itchy had mentioned tied him to the crime.

Her phone rang and she absently flipped it open. "Nelson."

"Detective Nelson, this is Jack Adams."

Molly's eyes widened and she lost her breath. She'd left a message for him earlier and spent half an hour thinking of what she would say. Now, she couldn't even remember the first three lines of her speech, designed to show off her professionalism and uncanny ability for police work. Jack Adams was a legend in the Phoenix P.D., but his role as Ari's father was far more significant to her. "Thanks for calling me back," she said automatically. "Sol Gardener thought you might be able to help me. I'm working on a case involving Vince Carnotti."

"Really? Well, it took a long time, but I knew that slime would surface again. Tell me the details."

She laid out the circumstances, describing Itchy's confession and his subsequent murder. "I'm looking at a guy named John Rondo, Carnotti's cousin. Does his name sound familiar?"

Adams sighed. "Maybe. There were lots of wiseguys and witnesses that came up. After Louie Noe was killed, we dug through Carnotti's life very carefully. I could have written that asshole's family tree by the time I was done."

She scribbled down the name. "Was Louie Noe the undercover cop that was killed?"

"Yeah. Really a stand-up guy. He'd gotten pretty deep into Carnotti's organization. We were just about to bring him out and use his evidence to nail Carnotti when he wound up in a Dumpster. Never caught the killer, and the investigation went

151

south after that."

Molly's pen stopped moving, and she noticed Adams's voice had faltered. When he offered nothing else, she assumed that his memories were tied to Ari and his wife. "So you got any advice?"

"I'd go back through Louie's file. That was 'ninety-three. Check my notes. I reference about five other cases in there, all murders and drug deals tied to Carnotti. Louie Noe's death was really the last piece. The trail went cold after that. It was almost like Carnotti packed up his operation, but he just went underground. I always thought there was a leak. Somebody was on the take and that's why Louie wound up dead. You solve that mystery, Nelson, and I'll owe you."

Molly brightened at the idea of being in Jack Adams's favor, particularly before Ari introduced them. "Thanks, Jack. You've been a big help."

Adams scoffed. "I ain't done shit. Biggest disappointment in my career was not catching Louie's killer. You need any more help or if you just want to bounce ideas, call me anytime. Got that?"

She smiled. She couldn't help but like him, despite his problems with Ari. "You bet. Thanks."

She hung up and went in search of Louie Noe's file. She nodded to a few rookies as she boarded the elevator and pressed "B" for basement. The doors opened to a dimly lit room and a damp smell. She knew this place had been forgotten each time the city remodeled the police station. There was never enough money, and since only Doug Dailey, the records manager, had to live down here every day, there weren't enough complaints to warrant action. She inhaled and it felt like a thousand mold spores clogged her lungs.

She flipped a light switch and noticed little change, except an extra level of gray washed over the room, exposing the maze of shelves and file cabinets. While much information was now stored electronically, she knew that boxes and file folders would always be a part of police work, and Doug would always have a job. She wandered down a row of filing cabinets, searching for the mid-'90s. The room was spotted in shadows, the fluorescent tubes poorly placed. It was the reason cops located the files and checked them out. A person could go blind trying to read in the bad lighting. She turned one more corner of cabinets and knew she was getting closer, having passed 1992. She twisted and turned with the aisle, realizing there was no real logic to the organization. Doug, who had been with the department for thirty-two years, merely added another cabinet at the end of the trail each time it was necessary, creating a winding gauntlet around the room.

Her eyes focused on the typewritten placards on the face of each drawer. She frowned when she realized the drawer she needed was at the floor level. She squatted and pulled it open, trying to balance herself and thumb through the manila files at the same time, which had been squashed together tightly. *Wouldn't want an inch of space to go unused*, she thought. Halfway through the drawer she found Louis Noe. She pulled out the thick file and checked the information inside. Jack Adams's name was listed prominently. She closed the file, just as a weird sensation drifted over her. She suddenly felt she wasn't alone. Her gaze swept down the row, but she saw no one. "Anybody here?" she called.

She listened carefully—and heard feet. They were hurrying to the exit. She grabbed the file and ran back through the maze. A few times she veered the wrong way, and she cursed under her breath. Just as she came upon the center aisle, the one leading directly to the elevator, she heard the polite ding and saw the doors close, on an apparently empty car.

Chapter Twenty-six
Thursday, October 19th
11:55 AM

"We're sorry we've wasted so much of your time, Ari. I guess James and I need to communicate better about what we want."

James and Rochelle Ferguson glared at each other, working to preserve a sliver of civility in her presence. James nodded stiffly in her direction and headed toward the car, not bothering to acknowledge his wife. Ari remained on the sidewalk with Rochelle, and the two of them watched James start the car and stare out the windshield. Ari could see the anger in his face from twenty feet.

"He's not usually like this," Rochelle said. "I thought he wanted to buy a house and start a family." Her voice trailed off in disappointment. When she faced Ari, tears streaked her cheeks. "We'll call you in a few days. I'm sure we'll be ready by then."

Ari watched Rochelle join her husband. He gunned the engine and the Corvette sped from the curb. She sighed, knowing it was unlikely they would call back. Another lost commission. Oh, well. She could always eat macaroni and cheese for a month.

They had bickered throughout the morning, James clearly annoyed that Rochelle had phoned a real estate agent. He barely noticed any of the homes, his gaze rarely leaving the floors as they previewed six different houses. Rochelle's attempts to involve him were answered with grunts or unenthusiastic comments of "That's nice."

Instead of purchasing a home, they would probably hire attorneys for a divorce. Ari had seen it before. Jane called it the "Homebuyer Hail Mary," when a couple made a last-ditch effort to resuscitate their marriage by joining together in a paper nightmare—a mortgage.

She retreated inside and heard Lorraine's exuberant laughter. Only one person made her laugh that hard, her eldest daughter, Lupe. Since Lorraine had started her family at such a young age, Lupe was more like a sister than a child. Ari paused in the doorway, and Lorraine motioned for her to come inside. She wrapped up her conversation, still laughing as she replaced the receiver onto the cradle.

"That daughter of mine has the most unusual life. A few guys came in for lunch yesterday while she was tending bar and asked her to be part of a commercial."

Ari's eyes narrowed. Lupe was incredibly attractive, and Ari's natural suspiciousness prickled. "Are you sure it's legitimate?"

Lorraine shook her head. "No, that's why I'm having them checked out, without Lupe knowing, of course."

"You wouldn't be calling Biz Stone, would you?"

"Yes. She's done some work for me in the past. Do you know her?"

Ari squirmed in her chair and she hoped she wasn't blushing. "I met her a few days ago. Jane hired her."

"Good idea. Biz is the best. I've known her for three years, and she's exceptional at what she does."

"Has she ever told you the story of how she changed her

name?"

"Yes." Lorraine's face melted into a puddle, and Ari thought she might cry. "So sad and far too familiar to me."

Ari knew that Lorraine's ex-boyfriend, the father of her children, had tormented her physically and verbally for years. "So, do you think Biz is the kind of person to hold a grudge?"

Lorraine chuckled and leaned back in her chair. "Ari, I would never want to cross that woman. She does tend to fixate, and she won't let go. If there's something she wants, she goes after it until she gets it."

Ari wondered if what Biz wanted was Jane—or her.

"Why are you asking? Is everything okay?"

She nodded, not wanting to involve her boss in the drama. "Yeah, it's fine. Hey, how do you know Teri?"

Lorraine looked up from her computer. "Oh, she works for Delores and Mitch Cavanaugh. I sold them their condo a few years back, and I met Teri. They call her their adopted niece. There's nothing she can't fix, and she's amazing with flowers."

"I met Mrs. Cavanaugh the other day. She was one of the florists we questioned."

"Well, I'm sure she isn't stalking Jane, but the woman knows her flowers." Lorraine reached for a contract on her desk. "Hey, has the Morales home inspection happened yet?"

"No, I was going to call."

"Good," Lorraine said.

Ari left her and went back to her office. She had much to do, but her thoughts wandered back to Teri and Biz. Either one of them could be harboring a grudge against Jane for her carefree attitude about romance. She pulled up Biz Stone's Web site, noticing it was nothing flashy, just basic information about the services provided. There were no pictures, which didn't surprise her. A PI craved anonymity. Biz didn't even mention her address, and all Ari knew was that it was located in the Sunnyslope area of Phoenix. She scrolled to the bottom of the screen, and her jaw dropped when she saw the name of Biz's Webmaster: flowerpower. It most likely was a coincidence, but she was tired of all the flower references that surrounded Jane's case. The suspect list was growing, not shrinking.

Her cell phone vibrated across her desk, and she realized that she'd forgotten to turn on the ringer after she finished with the Fergusons. "Hello?"

"Hey, babe."

Ari smiled at the sound of Molly's voice. "Hey, yourself. What's going on?"

Molly sighed. "We're going through files and trying to find leads. Um, I spoke to your dad last night."

Ari froze in her chair. "You did?"

"Yeah. Sol told me to call him about that case you mentioned. He was really helpful."

"Oh."

"Ari, I hope I'm not freaking you out. I just thought I should mention it in case your dad brings it up during one of his phone conversations."

"You didn't say anything about us, did you?" As soon as the words came out of her mouth, she instantly regretted her tone.

"Would that be so wrong?" Molly asked defensively.

"That's not what I meant, baby. You know that I intend to tell him about you, but he's not ready to hear it. He can't even figure out what to do about my birthday. You understand, don't you?" There was a long pause, and Ari could hear the police personnel in the background going about their day.

Molly sighed. "Yeah, I get it. I really do."

It was time to change subjects. "When will I see you tonight?"

"Probably later. I have to do a little shopping for somebody's birthday."

Ari smiled. She was off the hook. "Later is better than never. Are you coming to my place?"

"Won't Jane be there?"

"Not until after midnight. You know she's a total night owl,

157

and she's finishing the party plans with Lynne."

Molly chuckled. "Okay, I'll see you around nine."

"Great. See you then." Ari flipped the phone closed, thinking how easy it would have been to add *I love you* at the end of their good-bye. Her stomach rumbled and she decided to check her e-mail and run out for a bite. She whipped out a few quick responses to some of her clients' questions, most asking about the status of their transactions. She clicked on an unknown address with Happy Birthday on the subject line and was surprised to see a greeting card appear. She smiled, wondering which of her friends had remembered her birthday. A green button appeared on the screen and she clicked it to start the card, suddenly wishing she could rewind the action as she did it, since it occurred to her that she didn't recognize the address. The background turned to black and a white orchid materialized on the screen. She swallowed hard as the orchid grew in size until it filled the frame. Her attention was drawn to the center, where a speck of blood emerged and dripped down the petal. Almost as quickly as it had appeared, the entire picture dissolved and the e-mail disappeared. She found herself staring at her e-mail list again and wondering about the strange address. Gone was the original e-mail as well, and she doubted she would ever remember the address.

Her heart was beating fast as she picked up her phone and dialed Biz. The detective answered on the second ring. "Stone."

"Biz, it's Ari. Somebody just sent me a really weird e-mail card." She described the orchid and its disappearance from the screen.

"Do you remember anything about the address?"

"It was a series of letters and numbers, like something you would pick for a bank password, not anything you would want people to remember." She clicked into her Deleted folder and couldn't find it. "I assumed it was just one of those cute cards from the American Greetings Web site," she explained, suddenly feeling very stupid.

"It was encrypted and it was programmed to disappear after you read it, so it didn't leave a footprint. Whoever set it up really knows computers."

Ari thought of flowerpower. "You seem to know a lot."

"Some. I design my own Web site, and I took a few community college classes. I met this guy whose nickname is H.D., for Hard Drive. Don't ask what it means. He was the ultimate hacker, and he showed me a lot of tricks that have helped with my business."

"So do you think there's any way to trace where it came from?"

"Probably not. You might be able to run a Restore and find the e-mail, but my guess is that this person used a proxy server, which means that even a guy like H.D. would need a few weeks to dig around and find the original sender."

"Do you think this was some sort of virus? Is it going to harm my computer?"

"Not necessarily. I'm more concerned that you received it. I think it's fair to assume that whoever is stalking Jane may have fixated on you as well. Have you told Molly?"

Ari took a breath and realized she had erred. She should have called Molly first. This was a threatening message, and Molly would want to know. Yet she knew how busy Molly was with her FBI investigation, and she didn't want to worry her, especially since it was probably nothing, and she wasn't in any real danger. "I called you first about it since you're on Jane's case," she said, hoping she sounded logical. She really couldn't explain why she'd dialed Biz's number automatically.

"So you haven't told Molly."

"I'll tell her later. Look, Biz, what do you make of this?"

"I'm not sure, but somehow you've managed to catch the stalker's attention, possibly because Jane's living with you now. It could be that the stalker sees you as a threat, someone who could take Jane away from her."

What Biz said made sense. "Am I in danger?"

"Honestly, you might be, Ari. Getting a blood-dripping card on your e-mail isn't a good sign, and you should start an antivirus program immediately. I can come over and do that for you."

"Okay," Ari agreed, pleased at the idea of seeing Biz again for a professional reason.

"What happened at Jane's condo was an act of violence. Whoever is doing this is clearly getting very frustrated. I don't think we'll have to wait much longer for her to show herself. I'm thinking I need to shift my focus. I need to watch you."

She was grateful Biz couldn't see her face, which was burning and no doubt beet red. "Are you sure that's necessary?"

"Yeah, I'm sure. Does that make you uncomfortable?"

Biz's tone was caring and soft. The woman was one of the most straightforward people Ari had ever known. Somehow it always made her feel better. "Truthfully, it does. How am I going to explain this to Molly?"

"Well, give her a choice. Tell her that she can either burn some vacation days so I can keep looking at our suspects, or you *and* Jane are going to need stay close to me while we figure this out."

Ari knew Molly couldn't miss work during this investigation, but she had to tell Molly or it would violate their trust. She needed Biz's help, but a kernel of doubt about the PI's innocence still lingered. There were some incredible coincidences, and it was possible that Biz was the stalker. She debated the situation, knowing she had to trust someone.

She sighed into the phone. "Okay, you win. What do I need to do?"

Chapter Twenty-seven

Thursday, October 19th
2:18 PM

Paper covered nearly every surface of Molly's office. If Doug Dailey ever left his basement and walked in, he would flip at the sight of his precious files pulled apart and out of order, the information Molly and Andre deemed most critical now positioned at the front. Photos were tacked onto a portable board, and they had begun a chart of the players, Noe's name at the top and Itchy's at the bottom. Molly was certain a connection existed between the murders that spanned a twenty-year gap, and her gut told her that a dirty cop was at the center. Consequently, she and Andre had closed her blinds and locked her office door. They'd kept everyone away by invoking the term FBI. She had phoned Rasp, who was still answering to Washington about Itchy's death, but she agreed to come by later and help them find the links. Luck also had David Ruskin on vacation for the next week, and Molly knew she could work in peace.

They had started the morning poring over Noe's file, but Jack was extraordinarily meticulous about his notes, and over a dozen names of other investigations and murders were mentioned. The more she read, the more she liked Ari's father, whom she decided to call again later in the day to see what else he might remember. Each time they compiled a list of names, they trekked back to the basement to collect the files. She debated whether to share last night's incident with Andre, and as they headed down again, she told him about the hurried feet and the empty car.

"Are you sure it was empty?" He pointed to the area that housed the control panel next to the doors. "If someone didn't want to be seen, all he'd need to do is stand against the wall until the door shut." He demonstrated by hugging the corner of the elevator car.

"Why would he hide?"

"Maybe because he was following you. Everybody here knows about this case, and a lot of people heard you talking to Sol yesterday. If there really is a mole, you might have made him nervous. He might be worried you're on the right track."

The doors opened and Doug Dailey scowled when he saw them. "Again? You guys are emptying out whole filing cabinets." He pointed a finger and narrowed his eyes. "My files better be in order when they come back."

"They will," Molly said. "Don't worry, Doug."

They separated and went in different directions, hunting for various names in different years. Molly found herself in the same vicinity as the night before. She noticed that if she walked past a few more rows, she could peer down the aisle where Louis Noe's file belonged. She wondered if someone had been watching her. *Had she been in danger and didn't realize it?*

She pulled open a drawer and hunted until she found the file on Stoney Deprima, a small-time fence connected to Vince Carnotti. Deprima had been found inside his pawn shop, shot dead in 1994. Molly opened the file and stared at one of the crime scene photos. Deprima lay on the floor, a bullet hole through his forehead and a knife plunged through his heart, a paper with a single word pinned to his chest—*TRAITOR.*

She nodded, starting to feel the rush. Here was the connection. She skimmed the notes as she started back to the elevator. She met up with Andre in the center aisle, five bulging folders in his arms.

"I found it," she said, waving the file. "A case with the same MO."

They headed back to the office and cleared a space on her desk. Andre studied the crime scene photographs while she scanned the contents of the Deprima file.

She shook her head, irritated. "Who the hell investigated this? This is incomplete and the notes are shoddy." She flipped to the end of the official report, searching for the investigating detective's signature—and groaned. "David Ruskin. I should have known."

Andre glanced at her with a raised eyebrow, and she was certain she knew what he was thinking. Ruskin was a player in a Carnotti case then, and he was coordinating their efforts now. She read through everything inside the file and saw several parallels between Stoney Deprima and Itchy Moon. Both had petty records, neither had done major time, and both worked on the fringes for Carnotti—and both had died in exactly the same way. Ruskin had conducted minimal interviews and found no one to prosecute. She cursed when she thought of the difference between Jack Adams's cases and this one. Jack's files bulged with information, notes, ideas and pictures, whereas Ruskin's investigation of Stoney Deprima's death was completed with a handful of black-and-white photos and less than thirty pieces of paper.

"This just sucks," she said, dropping the file on her desk. "Anything with the crime scene photos?"

Andre shook his head. "Just shots of the vic from different angles. No real shots of the store or the bystanders who gathered. Not even any surveillance photos of investigative leads. It's like nobody cared if the killer was found."

"Maybe that's the point," Molly murmured half to herself. She stood up and walked around the room, glancing at the open files that surrounded them. There was nothing but dead ends.

A knock on the door made them both jump, and Andre peered through the blinds. A grin spread across his face, and he opened the door for Ari. She greeted him with a kiss on the cheek and a hello before turning to Molly, who could feel her insides doing flip-flops. The sight of Ari was enough to take her breath away.

"Hi, babe," Ari said, planting a quick kiss on her lips. "I'm sorry to bother you guys, but I really need to talk to Molly for a minute." They both looked at Andre, who winked and smiled before he left, pulling the door shut tightly behind him.

Molly only waited for the door click before she pulled Ari against her for a long kiss. "You're not bothering me, but this is quite a surprise."

Ari's finger wrapped around one of Molly's curls and she bit her lip. Molly frowned instantly. Anytime Ari bit her lip, she was carrying bad news.

"What's wrong?"

"Well, it seems that Jane's stalker may be fixating on me now, at least a little."

In a second, Molly felt her stomach tighten. "When did this happen?"

"Today. I got this e-mail and it was a little threatening."

She shook her head. Ari was clearly underplaying the problem so she wouldn't worry. "And what does 'a little threatening' look like?"

"I opened this e-mail greeting card and there was an orchid with blood on it, and then it just disappeared. No message. No real threats. Biz just thinks she should keep an eye on both me *and* Jane now."

Molly wasn't sure where to start. Fear and anger were fighting for her attention while her mind tried to let go of her thoughts about Stoney Deprima and Itchy Moon. She remained silent, processing her response, not wanting to upset Ari the day before her birthday or sound like a jealous bitch. "So Biz is going to make sure nothing happens to you? How is she going to do that?" She tried to look pleasant but doubted that she was successful.

"From a distance," Ari said, wrapping her arms around Molly's neck and letting their foreheads touch. "She's just going to keep an eye on me when I go out on appointments during the day. You're in charge of taking care of me at night, which means that we may need to suspend our usual routine for a while, and we'll have to be together every single evening." She kissed her, and they stared at each other. Molly couldn't help but smile when she got lost in Ari's green eyes. She found herself enjoying the idea of waking up with Ari every morning. Suddenly Ari stepped back, her expression serious. "I wanted to make sure I told you, because I know how busy you are, and if you could, I know you'd take care of me all of the time, but you can't. You've got to catch a killer. Do you understand that this is just business?"

Molly nodded, surprised to feel comfortable with the arrangement. "I'm just glad you told me. Biz is great at her job, and I know you'll be safe. Just make sure you check in with her. Don't take anything for granted, and most of all, you know that even though I'm stuck at work, if you need me, I'm there. This can all go to hell. I mean it." She locked eyes with Ari and stared at her.

Ari took Molly's hands and brought them to her lips. "I know, baby." She looked around the room, her gaze settling on the thin file. "Are you finding what you're looking for?"

Molly sighed and showed her their latest finding. Ari snorted when she saw the skeletal report David Ruskin had composed. Molly tapped one of the crime photos with a pencil. "I don't think this is a coincidence. This is how Carnotti sends messages to all of his people. Mess with me in some way, and I consider you a traitor. I believe that whoever killed Stoney Deprima also killed Itchy Moon."

"You mean John Rondo," Ari said.

Molly shrugged. "Maybe. I don't have anything to connect him to this murder nine years ago, and David Ruskin didn't even write down any leads."

"Do you think he's dirty?" Ari whispered. Although they were alone, to accuse a cop of forsaking the law was heretical, but they knew it occurred.

Molly didn't answer. She looked down at the floor for a moment, and when her eyes met Ari's, she knew Ari was thinking the same thing—Ruskin was the strongest possibility and might have been the doer for both murders.

There was a quick knock at the door and Rasp appeared. Her eyes went wide in surprise at the sight of Molly's arm wrapped around Ari's shoulder. They quickly separated and all three of them laughed nervously.

Ever adept at social graces, Ari stepped forward and stuck out her hand. "Hello. I'm Ari Adams, and I'm sure it's quite clear to you that I'm Molly's girlfriend."

Rasp laughed and nodded. "I suspected as much. Agent Connie Rasp with the FBI. I should tell you that your girlfriend is a great cop." Both of them smiled at Molly, who blushed appropriately. "If it wasn't for her, this investigation would have totally tanked."

"She's an incredible cop," Ari agreed. "Now, I really should get out of here so you can *continue* to be incredible." Ari grabbed her bag, kissed Molly and headed toward the door. She turned and said, "You know, you really should see if you can find John Rondo's girlfriend. Didn't you say he still goes to the High Life, even though he's married?"

"Yeah," Molly said. "The man's an asshole."

"I'd go talk to the girlfriend. See if she thinks he's an asshole, too."

Chapter Twenty-eight
Thursday, October 19th
4:13 PM

When Ari returned to her office, Biz Stone was waiting in the reception area talking on her cell phone. Their eyes met, Biz said good-bye, and she followed Ari to her office. "I want to take a look at your computer."

"I thought you said it was untraceable."

"It probably is, but it doesn't hurt to try. There's a function on your computer called Restore, and I might be able to find where the e-mail originated, but if this woman's smart, she's used a proxy server, and I'll hit a dead end. Then I want to show you some stuff I dug up on Courtney Belmont and Isabel."

"There's also another suspect," Ari said, thinking of Teri.

Biz halted and put her hands on her hips. "Another one?"

She nodded sympathetically. "Her name is Teri Wyatt. She does remodeling for Jane, but she doesn't have a strong motive.

She rejected Jane already, but she's connected to Cavanaugh Flowers."

"You mean the place we went to the other day?"

Ari nodded, and Biz shook her head in exasperation. She dropped into Ari's desk chair and pulled up her e-mail. Ari watched her click on several different screens that she either didn't know existed or never bothered to access. She knew how to create and delete messages and that was enough for her. After fifteen minutes of poking around, Biz leaned back in the chair, shaking her head. "I'd say this is definitely a dead end. I can't figure out where it came from. And your antivirus software isn't giving any clues either. I could have H.D. come over and take a look at it, but he told me it could take weeks to track down the proxy server. At any rate, you definitely need to install some anti-spyware software. I'm worried about keystroke loggers."

Ari's mind drifted to Biz's Web site, but a glance at her intense expression as she studied the screen gave Ari comfort. She couldn't imagine that Biz was staging a performance now, and her flirtations made it even less likely that she was the stalker.

"I don't think we have weeks. I think the stalker will reveal herself soon. She's getting impatient, and it's obvious that she's capable of violence."

"Let me show you what I've got." Biz grabbed her messenger bag and moved to the couch. She set two folders on the coffee table, one labeled Isabel Collins and the other Courtney Belmont. "Like I told you on the phone, Isabel is a prime suspect, but I'm not sure how Courtney figures into all of this." She picked up Isabel's file and withdrew several news clippings and some surveillance photos. "These clippings are articles about flower shows. She's won a lot of different awards in various categories, including orchids, and she's a respected horticulturalist. She even *created* a flower that I can't pronounce." All of the articles announced Isabel Collins as the winner of several prizes and praised her for her talent. "She lives in a gated community over in North Scottsdale," she said. "Her routine on most days is rather usual,

168

except for yesterday. She didn't go to work. I called just to see if she was there, and when I found out she wasn't, I headed over to her place and waited. The security guard and I are becoming buddies, and she was quite helpful."

"She?" Ari teased.

Biz colored and she wouldn't look at Ari. "It's all in the line of duty. Anyway, when her cute little red sports car finally passed through the gates, I followed her for a few hours. Her first stop was a pawn shop on McDowell. She was in there for about forty minutes and left carrying a small bag."

Ari's eyes shot up from the photo she was holding. "Was it large enough to hold a gun?"

Biz smiled in admiration. "You think so much like a PI, Ari. Why don't we go into business together?"

She frowned. "Why don't you stop flirting?"

The smile vanished and Biz cleared her throat. "Sorry. It's a bad habit I'm trying to break. After she left the pawn shop she went to the *Scottsdale Tribune* building near the Civic Center. She left with some papers."

"Probably taking an ad out."

"Maybe. Her last stop, though, was the most interesting."

"Where did she go?"

"She went to Emerson's. She was there for at least an hour and a half. I couldn't stay because I had another appointment, but I can't figure out what could possibly tie Isabel to Aspen."

"Maybe nothing. It could be entirely coincidental. A wealthy woman stops at an upscale restaurant for lunch. That might be the whole story."

Biz clearly didn't buy it, but she said, "Maybe. Now, Courtney Belmont is a mystery woman. I went through several search engines to find her in L.A., which was where she went after Albuquerque, right?"

"That's what the girl at the paper told me."

"Well, she didn't stay there very long." Biz opened the file, and Ari glanced through the downloaded newspaper and magazine articles written by Courtney Belmont. An article discussing how to clean your espresso maker, published in *Good Housekeeping*, included a photo of C. Belmont, and Ari studied the picture of a rather attractive woman in her early thirties with a short, dark pageboy. All of the articles were about food, either restaurant reviews or helpful hints in the kitchen. She saw the obvious connection between Aspen and Courtney.

Biz held up two different printouts. "As you can see, Courtney left L.A. These were written for two different newspapers, the *San Diego Tribune* and the *Yuma Daily Sun*."

Ari noticed the dates, which were four months apart. "Two months ago she was working in Yuma. She's clearly moving closer to Phoenix."

Biz nodded. "There are no other listings for the past few months. I'm not sure what Courtney Belmont has been doing lately, but I also checked all over Yuma. Her last known address was an apartment near the newspaper offices. The manager said she gave no forwarding address when she left. She had a month-to-month lease, too."

"So she wasn't planning on staying very long," Ari said, her gaze returning to the small photo. The eyes that met hers were self-assured and strong. There was nothing within the contents of the articles that would help. She put them back in the folder and set it aside. She relayed her conversation with Teri to Biz and showed her the picture on the Cavanaugh Web site. Biz sighed and rubbed her jaw. Ari knew what she was thinking. There were too many suspects. Biz went back to the couch and stretched her legs across the coffee table. She didn't ask permission to put her feet on the furniture, and Ari wouldn't have been surprised if Biz kicked off her work boots and took a nap. She looked good in her tight jeans and Heart concert T-shirt.

"See anything you like?" Biz asked seductively.

She looked away. *Damn!* She couldn't stop staring at Biz, and she was sending all of the wrong messages. "I was thinking," she said weakly. "Maybe the way to narrow the suspects is to think about my connection to Jane. If I'm being targeted as well, then who would have a grudge against me?"

Biz laced her hands behind her head and looked up at the ceiling. "I can't think of a single person."

"You're doing it again."

"Seriously, I think they all could have something against you. It's obvious you and Jane are incredibly close. I'm surprised you're not lovers, considering how you act with each other and the amount of time you spend together. Anyone who wants to be close to her could perceive you as a threat."

"But I don't have any romantic interest in her," Ari argued. "We're best friends."

"And how many friends become lovers? I've gone to bed with most of mine. Haven't you?"

The question disarmed her, and she had to admit that she'd dated many of her friends—except Jane. "Yes, but Jane's the exception. We could never be lovers. There would be too many explosions."

Biz laughed. "I can imagine." Her eyes locked on Ari's. "But you are missing out on some incredibly hot sex."

Ari heard the regret in Biz's voice, and the nagging doubt of Biz's innocence resurfaced. The sound of a car pulling up drew their attention to the doorway.

Jane eventually appeared, carrying a paper bag from AJ's Fine Foods. She smiled at Ari and turned to Biz. "Hey, this is a good surprise. Have you caught my stalker?" she asked with a grin.

Ari knew that on a superficial level, Jane was enjoying this attention. She probably recognized the risks, but the fact that she continued to hit the bars and bed total strangers suggested that she couldn't bend her ways, even when she was clearly in danger.

"Working on it," Biz murmured from the couch. "Don't worry," she added. "I'm not on the clock right now."

"What's in the bag?" Ari asked.

Jane smiled and looked inside. "Oh, nothing. Just a few things

171

I'm bringing along for the party tomorrow night."

Ari returned the playful smile and studied Jane, who wore an adorable pink-and-white checked dress with matching checked pumps. She tried to see Jane as others did. Her breasts were perfect, not too large and not too small. She had a terrific ass that looked incredible in a bikini, and Jane never missed an opportunity to wear a thong swimsuit. Jane was beautiful, and Ari thought of Biz's comment. *Could I ever be interested in Jane?*

Jane turned to Biz and pointed her finger. "You are coming, right? Either to work or hopefully just to party."

Biz nodded and Ari felt a lump in her throat. Molly would not be pleased to see Biz at the party—even if she was on assignment.

Jane noticed the files on the table and started thumbing through the information on Isabel. "I told you Izzie was amazing," she said, waving one of the newspaper articles. She opened the file on Courtney Belmont and froze. "Who is this person?"

"That's somebody who knows Aspen," Biz said. "Why?"

"Because I've seen her at Smiley's, and I think I slept with her last month."

Chapter Twenty-nine
Thursday, October 19th
6:03 PM

Molly and Andre fought rush-hour traffic to the edge of Phoenix. The High Life, a ritzy gentlemen's club, sat on Scottsdale Road, the dividing line between urban Phoenix and glamorous Scottsdale. The location afforded the strip club easy access to the richest clientele in Arizona and the lenient zoning codes of Phoenix. Valets dressed in tuxedos carhopped the BMWs, Mercedes-Benzes and Lexuses that strung around the building to the street.

Molly pulled into a spot and flashed her badge at an eager lot attendant already advancing toward them. At the sight of the shield, he raised a hand in submission and returned to his post while they proceeded through the thick double doors into the smoky main room. She didn't want to think about the amount of illegal activity occurring inside. She imagined the drug usage in the back rooms alone would be enough to shut the place down. They wandered through the gauntlet of cocktail tables, almost all of them filled with the after-work crowd, businessmen hoping to catch a little entertainment before heading home to the wife and kids. One man leaned over the stage, waving his money toward a gyrating dancer. His wedding ring glistened against the spotlight as he tucked the bill down the front of a brunette's G-string. Six dancers wrapped themselves around poles, moving to the blaring music and thrusting their mostly naked bodies toward the salivating men.

They had barely arrived at the bar when they were greeted by two muscular men in security polo shirts. One whispered in Molly's ear, "The manager will be out in a second."

She nodded, certain that the lot attendant had radioed inside, informing the staff that law enforcement was present. Within another minute an attractive redhead in an expensive suit appeared and shook their hands, introducing herself as Sandra Payton, the manager. They followed her down a hallway toward a massive oak door with a gold sign bearing her name. Unlike so many of the seedy strip joints, the High Life was highbrow, and Sandra Payton's office was larger than Sol Gardener's and smelled of expensive perfume. Molly sat down on a comfortable leather sofa, and her body melted into the plush cushion.

Sandra Payton sat across from them in a matching chair. She smoothed her finely manicured hands over her suit pants and gracefully crossed her legs. She painted herself as a classy business executive, but her breasts bulged against the seams of her dress shirt, which revealed much more cleavage than corporate America would ever allow. Molly couldn't help but let her gaze drift southward during the conversation. She was sure Ms. Payton was a former dancer who'd worked her way up the food chain.

"What can I do for you, detectives?" Sandra asked.

"We need to speak with one of your dancers," Molly said.

Sandra raised her eyebrows in inquiry and leaned back in her chair. "Who would that be?"

"John Rondo's girlfriend," Andre answered.

Her face drained of color and she sat forward, grasping the arms of the chair. "Has something happened to John? Is he all right?"

"He's fine," Molly said. "Well, as fine as someone can be with a possible murder charge hanging over his head."

Her eyes widened and she fingered the cross dangling between her breasts. "What murder charge?"

Andre glanced at Molly. "I take it you're rather close to Mr. Rondo?"

She smirked at the term and her eyelashes fluttered. "I'm his other half. I know he lives with Jennifer and the kids, but we've been together for twelve years, longer than that little Yale snob."

Molly instantly pieced the story together. John Rondo had married an upstanding woman who would give him credibility in the community while he continued to bed his girlfriend on the side. "Does Mrs. Rondo know about you?"

"Oh, please," Sandra said with a wave. "She counts on me to keep John happy. All she wants is the money and the kids. She's got the perfect life, and she can see whoever she wants."

"Is she having an affair, too?" Andre asked.

She smiled slyly. "In a sense. John's aware of her other life, and he's fine with it. There's no competition."

Molly shook her head. "What do you mean?" Sandra continued to stare at her, as if she should understand—and then she did. "So she likes women?"

Sandra's smile widened. "Very much, detective. Jennifer discovered her lesbianism in college, but she knew her wealthy East Coast family would disown her if she came out. Then she met John, who gave her the freedom to be who she was and the respectability to keep her family happy. All she had to do along the way was pop out a couple kids."

Molly sensed Sandra felt a level of appreciation for Jennifer

Rondo amid the disdain. "Have you ever been with her?" Molly asked.

Sandra looked away and recrossed her legs. "Jennifer and I experimented together a few times while John watched, but it never turned into anything. She's got her life and I've got mine."

Andre stood and went to a bookshelf. A few photos of Rondo and Sandra were prominently displayed. "Did he set you up here? Is this your life?" He gestured to the enormous office, disgust in his voice.

"There's nothing wrong with this life, if that's what you're implying," she said defensively. "I've got everything I need."

"Except the guy," Molly interjected. "You know he'll never leave his wife. You'll always be the other woman. That's got to bother you some of the time, doesn't it, knowing that he's out at a fundraiser or on vacation with the family when he could be with you?" She watched Sandra's foot bop up and down nervously while she fumed silently. "And Jennifer Rondo certainly can't complain. Talk about a woman who hasn't had to make a single sacrifice."

Her gaze snapped toward Molly. "What do you mean?"

"She gets it all. Family goes on vacation. Nanny takes care of the kids. They both meet someone in the bar afterhours and have a great romp in the sack before dawn. Then it's back to the perfect picture."

"John doesn't cheat on me," Sandra said evenly.

Molly leaned forward. "You're kidding, right?" She almost felt bad about what she did next, but it didn't stop her from reaching into her jacket pocket and withdrawing the surveillance photos the FBI had taken during the past week. She dropped them on the coffee table in front of Sandra and sat back in the lush leather couch.

Sandra stared at the picture closest to her, one of Rondo and a young blonde about to climb into a limousine. Curiosity forced her to pick up the pile and stare at her lover's other life. The second photo showed him at an outdoor café, engaged in a romantic conversation with a long-haired brunette. His arm was wrapped around her bare shoulder and she touched his cheek. Molly watched Sandra set the stack down, not bothering to flip through the rest of the photos, including one that depicted Rondo surreptitiously stroking the breast of a dancer at a competing strip club. She leaned back in the chair, her eyes downcast. When she looked up at Molly again, it was with resolve.

"What do you want to know?" she asked evenly.

"Tell us about his business dealings. Have you met many of his associates?"

"I've met lots of his associates, especially the ones from out of town. He brings them here for a good time."

"Have you ever met Vince Carnotti?"

Her face showed no sign of recognition. "Maybe. They're all Italian or have stupid nicknames, and they look like goons."

"Does he ever talk to you about what he does?"

She shook her head. "He doesn't talk about it, and I try to stay out of it."

Molly didn't believe her. She was too smart, and she'd been around Rondo too long. "You mean to tell me that after having a decade-long affair with the man that you've never overheard a phone conversation you weren't supposed to hear, or found him carrying a gun—"

"Or had him arrive at your place with blood on his hands?" Andre interjected.

Sandra looked away, her discomfort evident. Molly watched her struggle between the affection and the anger that were no doubt surging through her system. She picked up the pictures again, flipped through them and stopped suddenly. Molly glanced at the photo in her hand and saw that it was the one of the stripper. Sandra stared at it for a long time before asking, "May I keep this?"

Molly nodded. "Take whatever you want."

"This is all I need," she said slowly. She stood and went to her desk. She opened the drawer, dropped the photo inside and withdrew a key. "Yeah, there have been a few times when it's been obvious that John's been doing something he shouldn't."

She chose her words carefully, but she delivered the facts in a nonchalant tone, and Molly pictured her sitting in front of a grand jury. The woman could probably put Rondo away for the rest of his life. She walked to her filing cabinet and popped the lock. She searched for a file, smiled when she found it and took it to Molly. She was undoubtedly giving away something she'd been saving for a long time. The file was thick and filled with random scraps of paper and photos. A microcassette tape dropped in her lap.

"That's a conversation between John and some other guy about a hit in Florida. I accidentally recorded it when he picked up the phone one day after the answering machine already started. I decided to keep it for insurance."

Sandra's choice of words reminded Molly of Itchy, a man who always had an insurance policy. Sandra moved behind the bar and poured bourbon. Molly started flipping through the folder, amazed at the amount of notes she had compiled.

"Anyone care to join me?" she offered, holding up her highball glass.

They declined and watched her down one drink and pour another. She said nothing and only stared into the glass. Molly guessed she was reevaluating her whole life.

Andre continued to peruse the bookshelves. He picked up a framed photo and asked, "Do you know anyone named Itchy Moon? He was an informant that Rondo probably knew."

"Did he kill him?" she asked.

"Possibly. There was a meeting scheduled at Cactus Airpark not long ago. The informant never made it."

She froze with her drink almost to her lips and peered over the top of the glass. "Was he a young guy?"

"Sort of. Late twenties."

She shook her head. "No, the guy I'm thinking of is really young, like a teenager."

Molly and Andre exchanged glances. "Did he wear a hat?" Molly asked.

"Yeah, it's weird. I've never seen a kid in a fedora."

Molly scribbled in her notebook. "When did you meet this kid?"

Sandra brought her drink to the chair and sat down. She took her time with her answer, swirling the brown liquid in the glass. "I've seen him with John—never in the club," she added quickly. "Always outside. He always says hello to me." She chuckled. "He won't stop staring at my tits."

"Is he working for Rondo?" Molly asked, rather sure she knew the answer.

"I have no idea, and I don't want to know. I don't take drugs, and I stay as far away from John's business ventures as I possibly can. I'm operating a legitimate business here. I *own* this place. What's between John and me is personal."

Molly laughed. "C'mon, Sandra. You're in deep." She held up the folder. "You're a conspirator, and you've withheld evidence from law enforcement. You could go to prison."

Sandra continued to stare at the floor. Molly imagined she wouldn't fare well in a penitentiary and would become a rape target almost immediately because of her large breasts and comely figure. A silence ensued, except for the muffled strains of the dance music from the main hall.

"What do you need me to do?" she asked, finally making eye contact with Molly.

"We need you to make a statement," Molly explained. "We need you to testify against Rondo."

Her face crumbled as she recognized the ramifications of testifying against the mob. She most likely would be put into a witness protection program and forced to start a new life.

Andre approached Sandra with a photo in his hand. "When was this taken?"

"Um, about a year ago. John and I went to Paris for New Year's Eve."

179

He turned the picture toward Molly. At first she couldn't understand his interest. It was obviously taken at dinner and showed both Sandra and Rondo holding up Champagne flutes in a pose for the camera. She scanned the photo and settled on Rondo's chunky fingers wrapped around the delicate stem of the glass, a huge emerald ring adorning his right hand.

She turned the photo so Sandra Payton could see it and pointed to the emerald. "Does he always wear that ring?"

"You know, it's funny you should mention that. I asked him about it a few days ago, and he blew me off. Said he lost it. I was really surprised because that was his dead brother's college ring. It meant a lot to John."

Molly thought of the square impression on Itchy's bruised face and imagined Rondo's ring slamming against his cheek.

Chapter Thirty

Thursday, October 19th

7:18 PM

"I can't believe you slept with Courtney Belmont," Ari said. She passed Jane the catsup and watched her pour a perfect circle over her hamburger. While she carefully cut her meal into fourths, Ari chomped down on her sandwich and noticed their waitress eyeing Jane from the bar. They rarely stopped at Burger Betty's, Jane unwilling to dine at any restaurant without proper napkins and table settings after six o'clock.

Lost in her thoughts, Jane gazed across the restaurant. "Well, I think it was her. The face was the same, but the hair was different. It was lighter and longer." She paused and took a bite. "You know, the more I think about it, the more I remember that night. I really wasn't looking for a pickup." Ari raised an eyebrow and Jane feigned surprise. "Honest. I was tired, and it had been a long week. I'd had three closings and two difficult clients. On top of that, I think I'd already had a few dates with different people. I wasn't looking for action, just a quiet drink and a chance to watch the crowd. This blonde drops onto the stool next to me, buys me a few drinks, and pretty soon we're having a good time. It was really bizarre because I don't usually get drunk on kamikazies, but by my third, I was having trouble forming sentences and she was practically sitting in my lap. Vicky yelled at us to get a room, and the woman—Courtney, I guess—led me outside to her car. Everything's a blur after that. We went to her place, and all I remember is waking up in the middle of the night with a pounding headache. She was asleep next to me, and I tiptoed out. She never woke up."

"She didn't hear you?"

Jane grinned and winked. "Ari, honey, they never do. I'm the expert at the silent exit."

Ari rolled her eyes. It was no wonder Jane was being stalked. "What kind of car did she drive?"

Jane furrowed her brow and shook her head. "I can't see it. I was too far gone."

She thought about Jane's encounter with Courtney Belmont as they drove back to her condo. Jane was prattling away about her birthday party, certain that there would be photographers and reporters present from the *Echo*, Phoenix's local gay and lesbian magazine.

There was something about Jane's tryst with Courtney that wasn't right. Despite her tiny stature, Jane could hold her liquor, and Ari had upon occasion watched her guzzle five shots and remain sober. If three kamikazies sent her into a drunken stupor, there was more in the glass than triple sec and vodka. Ari wondered if Courtney hadn't slipped a drug into Jane's drink.

"Jane, did you ever get up to go to the bathroom when you were with Courtney?"

"Well, from what I remember, my friend Elise came by the bar and asked me to go over to her table to meet her new girl-friend. I wasn't gone for more than five minutes."

"Did Courtney go with you?"

"No, she said she'd save my stool. I'd already had a few drinks at that point, and I felt stone sober. I'm not sure what happened."

"I think she drugged you. How many times have I told you not to walk away from your drink? I'll bet that while you were gone, Courtney spiked your kamikazie with Rohypnol or a copycat drug."

Jane's face showed genuine disbelief. "Honey, I really doubt she felt she needed the date rape drug to get me to bed. I'm a sure thing. Everybody knows that."

"That's not the point." Ari took a deep breath, trying to control her anger. Jane didn't recognize the consequences of her lifestyle. "Date rape is about power, not how easy you are."

She looked stunned. "I've never thought of myself as being raped." Neither of them commented further, and Ari hoped she'd made her point.

She knew she'd failed when Jane pulled up to her building and left the engine running. No doubt her intention was to dump her and find someone who would take her home. Ari opened the door, eager for them to be apart. She loved Jane dearly, but it was conversations like these that reminded her of their clear differences.

Jane caught her arm. "Hey, I know you're only looking out for me, but you don't need to worry. I'm fine." Ari nodded, wordless. She couldn't change her choices. "Look, I love you, right?" Jane added with a friendly kiss. "I promise I'll be careful."

She squeezed her shoulder until Ari couldn't help but smile. There really was something about Jane's charm that was magnetic.

"Now, tell Molly I said hi and remind her to make more coffee in the morning before she leaves. As roommates you two leave a lot to be desired."

Ari nodded and pulled her long frame from the tiny car. She watched Jane speed away into the darkness and potential danger.

An engine started nearby and she instinctively turned around to find the source. Perhaps it was Biz. Parked cars lined the side street of the condo high-rise, but none pulled away from the curb. She felt a shiver down her back and moved inside quickly.

All she wanted was a shower and a glass of wine. Molly would be home in a while, and the idea of the two of them crawling into bed and watching a movie made her smile. She debarked from the elevator and her smile vanished as she approached her door. A long rectangular box rested against the doorknob, and she knew before she picked it up what she would find inside. There was no return address or markings on the plain brown cardboard and only a knotted piece of twine held it shut. She fumbled with her door lock, already noticing how light the box was, almost as if it was empty. But she knew it wasn't, and when she severed the twine with her kitchen knife and opened the box, she heard the distinct sound of tissue paper crinkling inside. The image of the bleeding orchid flashed in her mind as she parted the paper and found a single *Angraecum elephantinum*. She studied the flower, which still seemed so beautiful, and it was only when she glanced at the bottom of the stalk that she saw the note card and the handwritten message—*YOU DESERVE A REAL ONE AND SO MUCH MORE. HAVE A HAPPY BIRTHDAY.*

Chapter Thirty-one
Thursday, October 19th
7:49 PM

The mall seemed unusually crowded for a Thursday night to Molly, but she rarely shopped on a weeknight, so perhaps her expectations were low. Crowds were a good thing—it meant people weren't out on the streets breaking the law or causing car accidents.

She checked her cell phone, making sure she had a signal inside the mall. Andre had gone ahead to find Rusty while she made a quick trip for Ari's present. As important as the case was to her, she couldn't handle Ari in tears, which would inevitably happen if she didn't get her a gift. She cursed herself for procrastinating, longing to be with Andre when he found Rusty. She'd put off the shopping trip, having no idea what to buy for the woman she secretly loved but couldn't tell, at least not yet.

She wandered into a card store toward the birthday racks and suddenly felt overwhelmed by the sentiments and messages. She chose a sincere card and read the text inside, which gushed with loving phrases and even went so far as to use the exact word she was avoiding. She replaced it and stepped toward the funny cards, their covers plastered with cartoon characters, bright colors and outrageous scribbles. She didn't even bother picking one up, for she knew if she made a joke of her birthday, Ari would be upset, or worse—disappointed. She could handle her short and uneventful fits of anger, but she hated it when Ari was depressed. She sighed deeply, beginning to feel depressed herself, and exited the store to wait for her brother by the enormous fountain. If anyone would know what to do about Ari's birthday, it would be Brian. He was the most romantic man she knew.

"Hey, sis," his familiar voice called. He sauntered toward her, a small bag in his hand.

"What's that?" she asked.

"This is a present for Lynne. Our third anniversary of glorious partnership is coming up in a few weeks, and I'm getting ahead." He withdrew a rectangular box. Inside was a beautiful diamond pendant that Molly knew Lynne would adore.

"Oh, Bri, that's incredible. Lynne will love that. It's perfect." They both admired the necklace a bit longer before he returned it to the bag.

It all seemed so easy for him. *Why is this so difficult for me?* "I'll never find anything for Ari," she said.

"Of course you will." He put an arm around her and pointed at the nearby card shop. "Did you get a card?"

"Well, I looked, but all of the serious cards are too . . ." She paused and searched for the right word.

"Serious."

"That's it. I don't want her to get the wrong idea."

"And what idea would that be?" he asked, grinning.

She smirked. "I'm not ready. You know that. We've only been dating for six months. I need more time."

"I understand. Let's skip the card for now." He pointed at

186

a department store. "Let's try in there." She groaned and they went inside. He led her to the jewelry department and stopped in front of a display case of moderately priced gold and silver items. "Now, the key to remember is that there are certain things that one lover should never give to another. A blender comes to mind. Also, you need to know that there are levels of intimacy to gifts. Diamonds scream commitment, and they are a definite guarantee that you will indeed be in bed before the evening is over." He lifted his bag for confirmation just as an attractive saleswoman approached them.

"May I help you?"

Brian turned to her and smiled. "My sister needs a present for her girlfriend, one that shows how much she cares, but . . ." His sentence faded away and the saleswoman's red lips turned up in understanding.

"Of course. What you need is something that says thoughtfulness."

"Yes," Molly agreed.

"I'd suggest something in gold, possibly a bracelet or a necklace. There's always a watch, if you'd like to add an element of practicality."

She debated what would be the best choice for Ari. She'd seen her wear a number of different watches, so she probably had enough of those. The display case was full of necklaces with various thicknesses and designs. She thought some were attractive, but many were gaudy or ugly, and she knew Ari was rather picky about her jewelry. Her doubt increased the longer she stared into the case. She had no idea what to choose.

Brian apparently sensed her frustration. He pointed at a delicate gold rope that had a twist at the center. "May we see that one, please?"

"Excellent choice," the saleslady commented.

Molly chuckled slightly. She was already flirting with Brian. What woman wouldn't want a man who could select jewelry?

They examined the necklace, which seemed perfect. It wasn't

heavy and thick, so it wouldn't look enormous on Ari's dainty neck, but it wasn't so thin that it would go unnoticed and possibly break.

"Well, sis, what do you think? Does this necklace say I like you a lot? I hope you stick around?" He started to laugh and she playfully slugged him in the arm.

"It's not a diamond, but do you think I still have a chance for some hot and heavy sex?"

Brian's brilliant blue eyes twinkled. "I'd say the odds are in your favor."

Her cell phone vibrated in her pocket and she motioned to the saleslady while she answered Andre's call. "Hey."

"He's gone, Mol. The desk clerk doesn't know where he went, but his room is empty. I asked some of the other tenants, and they said he packed up yesterday and took off, said something about a cousin in California."

Molly stepped out of the store and into the mall to improve the reception. "That could just be for show. I think we spooked him, but my guess is that he's still around. He doesn't think we know about his connection with John Rondo."

"Then where is he?"

She glanced at the nearby storefronts and her eyes focused on a poster in Bob's Sporting Goods store. It depicted Phoenix Suns' star Steve Nash driving to the basket. "Is there a game at the arena tonight?"

Once the gift was purchased and Brian convinced her to buy a blank card and write her own message, Molly was on her way down SR-51, the lights of the arena in the distance. Rusty was a die-hard fan, and she doubted he would miss a game. She found Andre at the press entrance, and he introduced her to the head security guard, a burly man named Hugo. They circled the arena underground, stopping to chat with the various security guards who worked the entry points. They were only at their third stop when she saw Rusty as he turned and recognized her.

"Andre!" she shouted.

Rusty bolted into the crowd and headed for the main escalator. They followed behind with Hugo, who squawked into his radio, urging his staff to stop the kid in the fedora. They darted between the pockets of fans coming out early for halftime, and Molly knew if they didn't catch him before the entire crowd poured onto the concourse, he would vanish amid the thousands of people. They were gaining on him, and she watched as he ditched the overcoat and the fedora into a corner. On the jumbo screen she noticed only twenty seconds remained until the halftime buzzer sounded.

They continued around the concourse, Rusty occasionally throwing a glance behind him to check the distance that separated them. One hundred feet ahead was the main entrance, the place where thousands would descend momentarily. She heard the crowd count down the last ten seconds, and Rusty looked back once more—just as a blind woman and her companion emerged from the seating area. The woman's cane caught his ankle and both of them tumbled to the floor. Rusty jumped to his feet, but two security guards grabbed him immediately. They turned him around to face Molly, and the look he gave her was deadly. Her skin went cold, and she suddenly believed he was capable of murder.

"I'm not saying anything." He sneered.

Andre yanked one of the chains from around his neck. "You don't have to." Rusty cried out as the clasp broke, and Andre held up his fist. He opened his hand and presented Molly with a college ring—a square emerald stone in the center.

Chapter Thirty-two
Friday, October 20th
Midnight

The front door clicked shut with barely a sound and Ari sat up in bed, listening as Molly quietly moved through the living room. On any other night, Ari would be asleep by now; however, after opening the orchid, there was no way to turn off her brain. She had filed through the suspects, looking for a specific clue that would pinpoint the stalker. Her bet was on Aspen, simply because she believed Aspen was totally fixated on Jane and using the house hunt as a ruse to spend more time with her.

She listened as Molly emptied her pockets and went to the kitchen for a Scotch. It didn't matter what time she arrived home, Molly always ended her workday with a drink. Ari pictured her leaning over the counter, slowly sipping the Scotch while she processed the day and let it unravel at her feet. In a few minutes she would join her in bed, and Ari debated whether to tell her about the orchid, which she had hidden in her closet. She'd tried to call Biz, but the PI's phone went straight to voice mail. She had not left a message, knowing that she didn't want Molly walking into her condo and finding her with Biz.

She fell back against the pillows and heard Molly's footsteps nearing the bedroom. She shed her jacket and gun belt and stripped off her clothes. Always considerate, she slipped into the bathroom before turning on the light. The shower started, and Ari snapped on the bedside lamp and jumped out of bed to check on the hidden orchid. Molly rarely ventured into her side of the double closet since they didn't wear the same size and took no joy in comparing couture, but Ari didn't want her stumbling upon the long box before she could tell her about it. As she suspected, it had fallen over and was sprawled across her dress shoes. She stood it in the corner of the closet behind a garment bag she only used for traveling. When she was sure it was secure, she returned to bed and turned off the light just as Molly finished showering. She glanced at the closet, realizing that they were practically living together. Each had a drawer and closet space at the other's place, and there were many personal items that shuttled back and forth between Molly's apartment and her condo.

The bathroom light went out and Molly emerged still drying her hair, bringing with her the sweet smell of the jasmine shower gel they had found at the farmers' market. She discarded the towel into the hamper and crawled under the covers.

"Hey," Ari said, pulling Molly against her. "How was your night?"

"Mmm. You're awake. Everything okay?" Ari hesitated to answer, and Molly flicked on the lamp in response. "What's wrong?"

She couldn't lie to her when she was staring into her eyes. It was another reason she knew she loved Molly. "I got a package tonight that you should probably see." She went to the closet and brought the box to the bed. When she opened it, Molly's face fell.

"Shit. Whoever is doing this better pray that Biz catches her before I do." She put the flower aside and studied the note and the box. "No return address label, and this note is totally generic. No way to learn anything about the sender. The letters are block script and it's just written on a standard note card." She got out of bed and went to the living room. When she returned she was scribbling in her notebook. "Did the manager remember anything about when it was delivered?"

"It wasn't delivered to the front desk. I found it outside my door."

Molly's eyes widened and she worked to maintain her composure. The fact that the stalker knew where Ari lived and could walk to her door and leave a package was scary. Molly tapped her notebook and stared vacantly toward the wall. She was deep in thought, and when she looked up at Ari, it was as a cop. "I'll check all this out in the morning. Did you call Biz?"

It was a loaded question, and Ari worded her response carefully. "I left a message for her to call me, but I wasn't too worried because I knew you'd be home soon."

Molly nodded slowly and the moment of tension floated away. She took a deep breath and exhaled. "Well, there's nothing else we can do tonight, but *I'll* call Biz in the morning, and we can work on a game plan. I'm beginning to think something might happen at your party tomorrow night."

Ari thought of the note and the reference to her birthday. "Molly, you don't need to get in the middle of this. I know you're busy."

Her expression hardened. "I'm not that busy. You're my girlfriend, and you come first." She scooped up the orchid and the box and took them out of the room. When she returned, her expression remained serious. "I never thought I'd say this, but I'm going to tell Biz she needs to stay very close to you. We just got a huge break in my case, and I'm hoping we can wrap it up in the morning."

"That's great, baby." Molly slid next to her and they gazed at each other. Ari stroked her cheek, a cloak of security wrapping around her. Molly would never understand how she felt when they were together—safe, comfortable, loved.

"You know I'd be lost without you," Molly said, swallowing hard.

The words touched her heart. "I'm not going anywhere. You'll protect me."

Molly cocooned her in an embrace and she started to relax. She closed her eyes, feeling the wonderful rise and fall of Molly's chest against her back and Molly's warm breath caressing her skin.

Chapter Thirty-three
Friday, October 20th
1:15 AM

The gauge crept closer to empty, and she realized in a single evening she'd driven two hundred miles and blown almost half a tank of gas. After she'd left Ari's condo, she'd headed for the freeway and I-17, one of the few highways left in Phoenix where you could hit one hundred miles per hour and the likelihood of being pulled over was nearly zero. Once she'd passed the Pioneer exit, she'd accelerated to one hundred and ten. Only after she'd flown by the turnoff for Prescott did she realize how far north she was. She took the next exit ramp and hugged the shoulder. When she killed the headlights, blackness swallowed her. She breathed deeply, working to avoid the sudden claustrophobia that squeezed her chest like a vise. She looked down at her shaky hands and immediately clamped them onto the steering wheel for support, letting her head fall forward.

She closed her eyes and her mind returned to Hideaway and the stranger's words. *She'll never want you. All she wants is sex.* She pictured Jane with the femme, fondling and kissing each other. Jealousy turned inside her, and she thought she might throw up. She cracked a window and was comforted by the sounds of the nearby highway.

The stranger was right. Jane was not monogamous. She flirted shamelessly with everyone, slept with countless women— and then abandoned them in the middle of the night. And now she knew why. She'd seen it with her own eyes when Jane had dropped off Ari. The binoculars allowed her to watch not only their kiss, but Jane's hesitation, her desire. She was in love with her best friend, but she didn't know it. Every other woman was a substitute, a stand-in for what she couldn't understand about herself and what she couldn't have.

She lifted her head from the steering wheel and gazed through the windshield at the full moon. Awash in blues and grays, it shone bright, and she felt as if she'd been hit by a spotlight. She reached into the glove compartment and pulled out the gun. She felt its power in the moon's glow and studied the sleek, black metal barrel. She pointed it at the moon, imagining her target— Ari. Once Ari was gone, Jane would be free, and they could be together. She imagined herself in Jane's arms, lying prostrate on the couch at Hideaway. The thought made her smile.

Screeching brakes on the highway sent a jolt through her brain, and she sat up, realizing she was sitting in the middle of nowhere holding a gun. She tossed it back in the glove box and started the engine. She headed back to the city, toward the millions of lights that seemed to greet her. She jammed the gas pedal and watched the needle ascend to one-twenty. Tomorrow would belong to her, and Ari would have a birthday party she would never forget.

Chapter Thirty-four

Friday, October 20th

9:15 AM

Connie Rasp met Andre and Molly outside the Embers with a warrant in hand. "Itchy's DNA matches some skin found lodged in the ring's setting. That's all we need. I called Rondo's office, and they said he hasn't come in yet. His car is still here, and my surveillance team says he hasn't left. You two ready to make the collar?"

"Gladly," Andre answered, taking the warrant from Rasp.

As they rode up to Rondo's condominium, Rasp explained what had happened overnight after the FBI took Rusty into custody. "He may not have talked to you, but he sang for us once he realized he could go to prison for life. Seems Rondo recruited him to run drugs, and Itchy was along for the ride, trying to keep Rusty out of trouble. Itchy pleaded with him not to deal drugs, but the kid was determined. When you guys caught Itchy, he was actually holding for Rusty. He was the one who got Itchy killed.

He gave Itchy to Rondo after Itchy told him that he'd been arrested. Itchy told the kid that working with the police was the best way out."

"But Rusty didn't want out," Andre said. "He was in it for the money."

"Poor Itchy," Molly said. "He thought he could trust the kid. He saw himself as some sort of mentor."

Andre snorted. "That kid doesn't need a mentor. He needs a conscience."

"No doubt," Rasp agreed. "That boy is hard. I don't see a soul inside him."

"He sure had us fooled," Molly said. "He acts the innocent. I just wanted to throw my arms around that boy and help him." She suddenly remembered the other witnesses they had interviewed. "Did Rusty say anything about where Itchy got the wad of cash he was carrying? Or his comment about finding a meal ticket?"

Rasp shook her head. "Apparently Rusty really has no idea. What he told both of you was the truth, and he insists Itchy wasn't really involved with drugs. That part is still a mystery. There was something else going on with Itchy, and my guess is that it had something to do with that slip of paper. I just don't know if we'll ever figure it out."

The doors opened to the twelfth floor and two penthouse suites. They knocked on Suite A, but no one answered. They pounded and announced their presence, and Molly felt her heart rate quicken. Rasp called her team, who brought the manager up with a key. Molly worried that she would find a murder/suicide scene and Rondo would be dead after killing his family. When the manager arrived and opened the door, they only found one body—John Rondo. He'd been reading in bed and was shot twice in the chest. There was no sign of forced entry and nothing was taken. The FBI swarmed the building, and soon crime techs and agents were everywhere. Molly and Andre retreated to the lobby to stay out of the way.

"So where's the wife and kids?" Andre asked what Molly was wondering. "Why was he alone? What happened to his family?"

Molly shrugged. "I don't know. I just hope they're safe. I'm thinking somebody's worried that we're getting close."

"You mean the leak," Andre said.

Neither of them commented further, but Molly couldn't help but wonder if someone was covering his tracks. She thought Rasp was right and the slip of paper was a key piece. Itchy knew something, and he was killed for it. *What did he know?* Her mind returned to the night in the basement and the empty elevator, and the circles she'd been doodling. Everything was connected.

Thirty minutes later Connie Rasp appeared, shaking her head. "Okay, so the killer picks the lock, at least it looks that way. He uses a silencer, so nobody hears anything, and the night security guard said everyone was accounted for on the log. The video surveillance camera shows a pizza delivery man going up to the twelfth floor around ten, but the guy kept his face toward the floor. And the best part is that the night security guy remembered letting him up around the same time, but he was on his cell phone and really wasn't paying attention to what the guy looked like, except that he was white and wore a company baseball cap that shielded his face."

"Great," Andre said. "So nobody was with Rondo? Where was his family?"

Rasp smiled pleasantly. "The wife is away at a resort with the kids for a long weekend."

Andre snorted. "What about school? My mama never would have let me skip school for 'a long weekend.' What's with these parents nowadays?"

"They're very indulgent," Rasp said.

"When was he killed?" Molly asked.

"M.E. guesses between nine and midnight last night."

"That lets Rusty off the hook," Andre said. "And it looks professional."

Rasp glanced at Molly. "Where do you think Rusty fits into

198

all of this?"

Molly shrugged. "I doubt he killed Rondo." Rasp said nothing, but Molly knew she was thinking about the mole.

The main doors flew open and a beautiful blonde hurried through, accompanied by Sandra Payton. Molly's jaw dropped at the sight, and Andre touched her arm. "Is that who I think it is?"

"Yup. I'd say this mystery just got interesting."

Rasp went to meet Jennifer Rondo, who started to cry when Rasp broke the news. Molly noticed that Sandra remained stoic, and at one point, their eyes met, but her expression didn't change. Two agents took Jennifer Rondo to the building manager's office for questioning, and Sandra joined Molly and Andre.

"Detectives, what are you doing here?"

Molly offered a pleasant smile. "We were here to arrest John Rondo for murder, but someone's saved us the trouble." Sandra shook her head, and Molly realized she wore a sundress, as if she too had been enjoying some time by the pool. "So how is it that you're with Mrs. Rondo? And where are the children?"

"The children are with friends now. We didn't want to bring them here after the police phoned Jennifer."

"And why are you here?" Molly pressed.

"After you showed me those very interesting photographs, I phoned Jennifer. She told me that she had taken the kids to the Pointe at South Mountain for the weekend. The kids were off today because the teachers had a professional workday. I asked her if I could come by. I had some information she might like to see."

"Why would she want to see that photo?" Andre asked. "You said that she didn't care."

Sandra drew a long fingernail across her forehead to replace a random strand of hair that had freed itself from her loose bun. "She doesn't, but I did. She saw how hurt I was, and she comforted me. It was quite lovely."

Andre scratched his head. "So you and Jennifer Rondo spent the night together?"

"We did," Sandra said with a wicked smile. "We spent most

of the evening playing with the children, and after they went to sleep, we ordered room service and went to bed. It was really quite domestic."

"What time was room service?" Molly asked.

"Somewhere around ten, I'm not sure. If it's that important, I'm sure the bellboy will remember. He saw both of us, and we gave him a generous tip, and a little bit of a show as well." She laughed and her cheeks reddened. "We were definitely in the throes of passion."

Molly laughed in disbelief as she pieced together the murder of John Rondo. "I have to tell you that I am incredibly impressed."

"Whatever for, detective?"

"You've protected yourself and Jennifer Rondo with airtight alibis, killed off the man who scorned you and bedded his soon-to-be extremely rich widow. That's amazing."

Sandra feigned innocence. "Detective Nelson, you are correct that Jennifer and I are pursuing a relationship, and we most definitely can account for our whereabouts last night, but I assure you that I don't know anything about John's death."

Molly leaned close enough to smell Sandra's perfume. "You're telling me this is all extremely coincidental?"

"And very fortuitous," Sandra added. "I hear the Witness Protection Program is really a drag."

The office door opened and a teary Jennifer Rondo emerged with Rasp. She went to Sandra's open arms, and together they walked out of the Embers and into a convertible Jaguar. Andre's cell phone rang, and he wandered over to a corner. Rasp motioned to Molly, and they exited a side door into a small garden and found a bench overlooking a koi pond.

"Her alibi's solid," Rasp said.

"She didn't do it."

"What about the other woman?"

Molly shook her head. "She may have set it in motion, but it was a pro. I'm guessing that she used one of Rondo's goons to help her out. She knew a lot of his friends, and I'll bet there were a few willing to do anything for Sandra. Go ahead and subpoena her phone records, but I doubt you'll find a trail. She's too smart. She had her own personal motives for wanting him dead."

"Hell hath no fury," Rasp said.

"Well, that and the fact that she avoided the entire judicial system as well." The wheels turned in Molly's brain. "There's one thing that bothers me. Sandra Payton may have wanted Rondo dead, but she was also the only one who knew about our investigation and Rondo's tie to Rusty."

Rasp sighed. "If that's true, and she happened to tell someone connected, then Rusty could be in danger, too."

Molly nodded. "He could, but I don't think he knows anything else."

"That doesn't always matter. Since I've started this investigation, I've learned that Carnotti doesn't take chances. Anyone who gets in his way winds up dead." They sat in silence watching the three large fish swim in circles around the tiny pond. "You did great work," Rasp said.

Molly shrugged. "Yeah, but we lost Carnotti."

"Not necessarily. Something might eventually come out of that file you got from Sandra Payton."

"Maybe." She glanced at Rasp, realizing the woman was watching her. "So do you go back to D.C. now?"

"For now, but I'll be back if something turns up."

Molly held her gaze but didn't know what to say. If it was a different situation, and if neither of them was involved, she was sure she would be asking Rasp to stay a little longer in Phoenix. But she was involved, and she loved Ari. And Ari trusted her. The moment dissolved when Andre burst through the door, still holding his cell phone out.

"What's wrong?" Molly asked.

"Rusty's dead. Guard found him swinging from a pipe in his cell. Hung himself with a belt."

"Don't they take away their belts?" Rasp asked.

Andre nodded. "Yeah, they do. Somehow he got one."

Chapter Thirty-five
Friday, October 20th
4:00 PM

The sun stretched downward, and Teri felt the relief of a cool breeze by four o'clock. Although the Phoenix temperatures were still in the high eighties, nights were coming sooner, and she welcomed the break from the heat, particularly when she was outside laying pipe or up on a roof slapping down tar. The only time she didn't mind was when she was doing landscaping or working at her aunt's shop. She didn't seem to notice the sweat dripping down her back when she was planting or watering, even in the middle of July. The explanation was easy. Construction was her job, but horticulture was her passion. She loved flowers and plants, and someday she would save enough money to go to school and get her degree, not that Aunt Delores thought she needed one. She'd worked in greenhouses most of her life, and Aunt Delores had won several prizes at different flower shows because of Teri's knowledge and passion.

She transferred the three-gallon rosebushes from the wagon to the wooden palette where they would sit until they were purchased. She smiled proudly. She'd grown them herself, and while she didn't like roses as much as orchids, she had to admit the Escapades were beautiful. Their rich purple petals would surely attract buyers.

She finished unloading the roses and headed back to the greenhouse. She wanted to check on her prized possession and prepare it for travel. She planned to give it to Ari for her birthday that night, and she hoped that Ari would have the same appreciation for it that she did. She heard the chime of her cell phone indicating a text message was waiting. She pulled her phone from her pocket and smiled at the message—*I need another orchid.*

Chapter Thirty-six
Friday, October 20th
6:20 PM

When his cell phone rang, he was just pulling up to his house at 6815 Moon Avenue. The theme from *The Godfather* filled the car, announcing the caller, Vince Carnotti.

"Hello, Vince."

"Are things under control?" Carnotti asked, suspending a civil greeting.

"Everything's fine. It all worked out, although we lost John."

"John became a liability. He and that teenager had to be eliminated."

"That's true."

"What about you? Can I count on you?"

"Of course. I can't believe you feel you need to ask. We've worked together for years, and I don't think I've ever given you a reason to doubt my loyalty. Arizona's always been easy, hasn't it?"

"I know, I know. I'm not suggesting you're slacking, but it's getting tighter. More questions are being asked. Those two dykes, Nelson and Rasp, they came very close to the truth this time."

"Trust me. You don't have anything to worry about. I've got a plan."

Carnotti sighed. "I do trust you, but it's my neck—"

"Don't worry. Rasp is out of here, and I'll make sure Molly Nelson never bothers us again."

There was silence on Carnotti's end, and he knew Vince was weighing his loyalty, his ability to deliver.

"All right. Have a pleasant weekend."

The line went dead and he pocketed the phone, his hands shaking slightly. He gathered up the groceries from the passenger seat and trudged to the house. When his gaze landed on the large iron house numbers, he smiled, thinking of Molly Nelson and Connie Rasp spending hours listing the numeric possibilities on their white boards, surfing the Internet for clues to the paper that Itchy had left.

The little weasel had thought he was so smart writing down the address, not bothering to include a street name for added protection. If it was randomly discovered, no one would realize what it was with only the numbers. And Itchy didn't need to write down the street name since it was easy to remember—his last name.

But Itchy was gone, fortunately before he ruined everything, before he told his secret—before he revealed the mole. Itchy's attempted blackmail scheme was ill-fated, and while he admired Itchy's boldness, he knew there was no way Itchy would have ever reaped more than the few hundred dollars he'd been given to shut up. Itchy got greedy and wanted more, threatening to reveal the mole, *him*. That was his mistake.

He shifted the bag of groceries on his knee to get the key in the lock, recognizing that although Nelson had not figured it out, Carnotti was right. She had come close—too close. She needed to be neutralized, and he really did have a plan. It would take months to unfold, but in the end, Molly Nelson wouldn't be an issue anymore. There was no way that she would jeopardize everything he had worked for, everything he had earned—the expensive home at the base of Mummy Mountain, his wife's Mercedes, and the Cayman Island bank account that would eventually supplement his retirement as a civil servant. As a cop, he'd realized early on that he could never live on a basic salary, but he relished power and the way his badge opened doors and presented opportunities. Soon, his years of climbing up the ladder would pay off.

He'd fed Nelson and Rasp the trail of crumbs they'd followed, all the way to John Rondo's door. He regretted Rusty's death. That kid was sharp, and it was unfortunate he couldn't have been protected. He was smarter than John ever had been.

As he set the groceries on the counter, he took a deep breath. He'd escaped a bullet. He nodded in resolve. It was time to put the plan in motion for Molly Nelson. A twinge of guilt hit him, but it was gone in a second. It was always hard to bring down a cop, but this was all about self-preservation and survival.

And he would survive.

Chapter Thirty-seven
Friday, October 20th
7:55 PM

The day had blown by with appointments and paperwork, and Ari had little time to think of anything except her job. She was floored when the Fergusons showed up at her office unannounced, asking to preview more houses, but she was elated when they actually found one they wanted to write an offer on. When Ari asked Rochelle what had happened, she smiled and mentioned the power of feminine wiles. Ari had hardly thought of the stalker, and Biz had been close by all day after Molly had a half-hour discussion with her on the phone. Jane was safely cloistered inside Hideaway preparing her party with the help of one of Biz's associates—a rather large man named Biff.

Her anxiety grew as the workday ended, and by the time Molly picked her up for the party, her nerves were raw, and she was convinced that the stalker would make some sort of show in front of Jane at Hideaway. Biz assured her that she would be watching in the shadows, but Ari was only half comforted since she didn't know for sure that Biz wasn't a suspect herself. Her gut told her that Biz was not the stalker, so she let her suspicions slowly evaporate. She needed Biz's help, and the only alternative was to involve Molly—an option that was clearly a last resort.

She greeted Molly at the door with a quick kiss and a long look up and down the detective's body. Molly wore a Western shirt, tight jeans and cowboy boots. "I see you have your lariat. Where's your hat?" Ari teased.

"Out in the truck. I'm supposed to be Annie Oakley." Molly held out a box for her. "And this is for you."

"What is it? Is this my present?"

Molly offered a sly grin. "Sort of. It's a present for me. It's from Jane. And you're to put it on for me right now."

She took the package to the dining room table. A quick glance at the contents told her what she needed to know. While Molly would spend the evening as Annie Oakley, she would be dressed as Wonder Woman.

"Oh, my God. Honey, I can't wear this!" Ari held up the red boots in one hand and the tiny red, white and blue outfit in the other. She frowned at the sight of Molly's open mouth. "You're a big help."

"Baby, I am not going to get in trouble with Jane over this. And frankly, it's every lesbian's fantasy to have her girlfriend dress up as Wonder Woman."

Realizing she would never win this argument, she excused herself for a few minutes to the bedroom and emerged wearing very little. She watched Molly's gaze probe her body and was pleased to see it settle on her red and gold breastplate. "Well, how do I look?"

Molly sauntered up to her and placed the lariat over her head. She cinched the loop around her waist and pulled them together. "I'm bringin' you in." She buried her tongue in Ari's mouth, eliciting little sighs of pleasure from her.

Ari pulled away and cupped Molly's face in her hands. "I'll make you a deal. We skip the party and you can have Wonder Woman all to yourself. I'll even let you tie me up with my golden lasso, and you can ask me anything you want. I won't be able to lie."

They looked down at the coil of rope attached to Ari's waistband, and Molly swallowed hard, clearly tempted. "You know how much I hate parties, and you know how much I love being alone with you, but I've been threatened with death by Jane, and Brian has said I'll be disowned from my family if I don't get you to that party. So we need to go right now before I change my mind."

Molly pulled her lariat back over Ari's head and walked to the door. She held up a long coat for Ari, who slipped it on over the costume.

"I can't believe Jane got you to dress up."

Molly shook her head. "Jane didn't get me to do anything. I picked this outfit and told her it was nonnegotiable. She had a much different costume in mind."

"Oh, really, what was that?"

"Xena."

Ari could hear the blaring music from outside Hideaway. Molly took her hand and led her through a darkened hallway. A hatcheck girl took her coat and directed them to follow the glow-in-the-dark female symbols on the ground. They rounded a corner and a blinking arch announced, "Girl Power" in colorful lights. Through the arch they found a living tribute to herstory. Posters of famous women hung from the ceiling. Ari easily recognized Shirley Chisholm, Rosa Parks and Indira Gandhi. Large cutouts surrounded the tables, including Marilyn Monroe, Olive Oyl, Maude and Batgirl. A waitress dressed as Rosie the Riveter sashayed past them carrying a tray of cosmopolitans.

"Jane has really outdone herself," Ari yelled over the music, a

Madonna dance mix.

"It's all for you, baby," Molly said, kissing her on the cheek. "Hey, there's Brian and Lynne."

Dressed as Cleopatra and Marc Antony, they waved and made their way through the crowd. Lynne threw her arms around Ari and gave her a big hug. They were still exchanging greetings when the music stopped and the lights went down.

"What's happening?" Ari asked, panicked, suddenly thinking of the stalker.

"I think Jane found out you're here," Molly whispered.

A fanfare of trumpets broke the silence and Jane's voice boomed throughout the room. "Ladies and gentlemen, our guest of honor has arrived. Please welcome Ari 'Wonder Woman' Adams!" The crowd roared and a spotlight blinded Ari. Jane appeared dressed in a leopard skin thong bikini and escorted both her and Molly to the DJ stand, a replica of a '50s jukebox.

"Do you love my outfit?" Jane asked.

"Who are you supposed to be?"

"Jane, of course!"

Ari rolled her eyes and followed Jane's instructions to stand in front of the crowd. Jane held up her hands for silence and shook her breasts, which only made the guests cheer louder.

Eventually the noise fell to a drunken murmur and she shouted into the microphone, "Okay, now, before I ask Ari to make a speech, I need to present her with a gift from her father." Jane's whole face smiled, and Ari felt herself blanch. Ever the actress, Jane jumped off the dais and headed to a corner of the bar, the spotlight following her the whole way. A blue velvet curtain hid the gift from view, and Ari watched her grab the red cord that extended from the ceiling. "Ari, your dad told me to tell you that he debated long and hard about what to get you, and he thought this was something you could really use."

"Oh, God," she whispered to Molly.

"Get ready for anything," Molly replied.

"Here is your present!" A drum roll echoed throughout the

room and Jane yanked the cord. When the curtain fell to the ground, Ari couldn't believe what she saw—a motorcycle.

The crowd laughed and cheered while she stood frozen, too stunned to say or do anything. It was obviously very expensive, that much she could guess. The beautiful chrome glistened against the harsh spotlight, and she admired the sleek black paint. She felt Molly's arms wrap around her middle.

"Are you okay?"

She nodded slightly, her eyes still focused on the machine and Jane, who had mounted the motorcycle and was playing to the crowd. "What am I going to do with that?"

"I don't care if it ever leaves your house, so long as you let me buy you a leather biker's outfit."

"Very funny."

Jane ran back across the room and thrust the microphone in Ari's direction. "Okay, Ari. It's time for you to say a few words. What would you like to say to your adoring public?"

The crowd chanted her name and she cleared her throat. "I just want to thank Jane for this amazing party, and I thank all of you for coming. Please have a wonderful time." She quickly handed the microphone back to Jane. "I hate talking in public," she murmured into Molly's ear.

"Trust me, baby. No one will remember a word you said. They were all too busy staring at your costume."

Ari turned to escape the dais, but Jane grabbed her arm. "Not so fast, my fabulous best friend." She waved at the crowd again and pointed to the bar area. "Okay, now before we all get too sloshed to appreciate a true work of art, I would like everyone to turn their attention to the magnificent cake coming toward us!"

Ari's heart skipped a beat as she watched a chef push a cart across the room, dreading to see what pornographic image Jane had captured in sugar and frosting. Ari was instantly relieved to see that the cake appeared to be flat and rectangular and didn't resemble any part of the female anatomy. When the cake pulled up in front of her, she saw it was covered in computerized images of her—fishing with her father, drinking with Jane and kissing Molly. She choked up when she studied the picture in the middle: her mother, standing outside the Orpheum Theater on the day they saw *Annie*.

"Do you like it?" Jane asked tentatively.

Ari threw her arms around her best friend and kissed her. "I love you. You know that, right?"

"Yeah, honey. I know."

"Where did you get some of these pictures?"

Jane smiled, tears in her eyes. "Your dad sent them to me." Ari couldn't speak, suddenly overwhelmed by conflicting emotions. "Just go have a good time, okay?"

She nodded. Molly guided her to a group that included Lorraine, Lupe, Andre and Teri. They all said hello, and Andre tapped Molly on the shoulder.

"Mol, do you know Lupe, Lorraine's daughter?"

Ari noticed Andre wore a huge grin on his face, and Molly chuckled in response. There was clearly an inside joke that she didn't understand, and judging from everyone else's reactions, they didn't either. Even Lorraine smiled pleasantly as Andre wrapped his arm around Lupe's waist. They were definitely becoming friendly.

"It's nice to meet you, Lupe," Molly said.

"C'mon, sugar, let's dance." Andre and Lupe headed toward the dance floor, but Andre turned around and shouted to Molly, "I'm a big fan of McGurkee's hoagies!" He joined Lupe in a bump-and-grind dance that Ari doubted Lorraine would enjoy watching.

"What was that about?" Ari asked.

Molly sighed. "Nothing. Why don't I grab us some drinks?" She pecked Ari on the cheek and disappeared toward the bar, leaving her with the group.

"You look amazing, *chica*," Lorraine said, kissing her on the cheek. She was dressed as Mae West, complete with a huge blond wig and push-up bra. Her chest was practically falling out of her skintight evening gown. She twirled around for Ari to see. "What do you think? I'll bet we'd get more clients in these outfits."

Everyone laughed and Ari blushed. She turned to Teri, who greeted her with a pleasant smile. She wore a pair of mechanic's overalls and a baseball cap. "Hi, Teri. I'm glad you could make it."

Teri leaned toward her and whispered in her ear under the music. "Thanks for letting me come. I know we just met, but after everything Jane's said about you, I feel like we know each other really well."

Ari nodded and stepped away, unsure of Teri's meaning. She wandered to another table, talking to the guests. She was amazed at the turnout and didn't realize how many friends she really had. Of course some clients had come, but many of the guests were women she'd known for years throughout the community. They offered their hugs and some commented on her costume, but a few made bold come-ons that she was glad Molly did not hear. She glanced around and found Jane dancing on one of the tables with a tall Latina. Her anxiety lowered at the sight. As long as Jane was up there, Biz could keep an eye on both of them—wherever she was.

Molly returned with their drinks and they visited with their friends, moving from table to table, accepting hugs and birthday kisses. Molly stayed close, her hand often at Ari's waist. Everyone could tell they were a couple, and Ari liked the fact that Molly let everyone know it once in a while. She would whisper in her ear or caress her cheek. They were gestures of intimacy, gestures of unspoken love. After they both had downed a few drinks, they braved the dance floor and spent several songs looking into each other's eyes.

Ari finally remembered to check on Jane, who was sitting at the bar doing tequila shots with three women dressed as Xena. She laughed and pointed for Molly's benefit.

"I guess she found the warrior princess group," Molly said. "I know what I've got." Molly gazed into her eyes, and she thought her lover might utter the words, but instead Molly just smiled and pulled her tighter.

She closed her eyes. She thought she might cry, but she willed away the tears. Molly would never understand. "I need a restroom break," she said and quickly excused herself before Molly could notice her expression or follow her. What she needed was to be alone.

She skirted along the edges of the crowd, determined not to be stopped for conversation. Fortunately she knew she could avoid a long line by using the manager's private bathroom. She cut through the infamous back room and headed into an adjoining passageway. She stepped inside the manager's spacious office, letting the door shut behind her, and sat down on the couch. Her feelings for Molly were overwhelming and it was becoming unbearable. She knew now that she couldn't remain in this holding pattern. Things had to change, and she was determined to say something that night. If it meant that the relationship exploded, then that's what would happen. She decided action trumped inaction.

Just as she made her decision, a gloved hand covered her mouth. "Don't say a word," the stalker whispered.

Molly watched Ari's backside head for the manager's office. She knew Ari was upset, and she guessed that it had something to do with their relationship. She started to worry, feeling as though Ari was slipping away with every step she took down the hallway. She knew she had missed a perfect opportunity. She could have said the words, but every time the right moment came, her tongue folded into a pretzel and she couldn't speak. She needed a drink, and Vicky was ready with a Scotch.

"Your girlfriend looks totally hot," Vicky said.

She shot her an icy stare and Vicky held up her hands. "Hey, I'm just observing and admiring, Molly. I'm not touching."

She gulped the Scotch and scanned the bar for Brian. With

Ari out of the room, she needed an anchor. Spotting him at a corner table with Lynne, she pulled herself off the stool and waved the glass at Vicky.

"You know, Vicky's right."

She turned to Biz Stone. The PI was all in black, slouched over the bar a few stools away. "Shouldn't you be watching Jane?"

Biz pointed at the DJ booth, where Jane and the DJ were fastened in a liplock. "I know exactly where Jane is. Where did Ari go? I figured you'd be upset if I kept an eye on her."

Molly narrowed her eyes and leaned over the bar, feeling the effects of the five Scotches she'd consumed. "Damn straight. But even before Ari got that orchid, you've been coming on to my girlfriend."

Biz shrugged and swirled the straw in what looked to be sparkling water. She stared at Molly, who suddenly felt very vulnerable and inept. She didn't want to get into a competition with Biz. She knew she would lose. Biz crossed the distance between them and took the stool next to her.

"Nelson, look. You don't have anything to worry about. I'm not after Ari. She's made it clear to me that she's in love with you."

Molly faced her. "Why would you say that?"

"Because she told me."

She made no attempt to hide her shock. "What?"

"I take it she hasn't told *you* yet, huh?" She looked down. "Look, Nelson, I'm easy to confide in, so Ari took advantage of me."

She snorted. "Stone, Ari didn't take advantage of you at all." She pointed a finger at her. "I know you a hell of a lot better than Ari, don't forget that. I know who you are. I know *what* you are, and don't think for a second that you have any chance with her. God, if Jane knew you came on to her, she'd have a fit."

Biz playfully grabbed her extended finger and brought it to her lips. "Yeah, Nelson. You're right. You know me. You've got my number. But here's what you need to understand. Your hot

215

girlfriend? She told me that she loved you before she even bothered to tell *you*. You need to think about that. Ari's not going to wait around for eternity."

Biz scanned the dance floor and Molly followed her gaze—Jane was starting a conga line. Biz sauntered away, leaving Molly with a huge emptiness in her heart that was rapidly filling with anxiety. Biz was right. Ari wouldn't wait forever. She finished another Scotch for courage and went in search of Ari. It probably wasn't the ideal moment to pour her heart out, but timing no longer mattered.

"I want you to know that I have a gun at your side, and if you scream, I'll shoot you," the stalker whispered gruffly.

Ari gave a slight nod and remained still. She could feel the woman's breath against her ear, ragged and heavy, as if she were afraid. Ari's eyes shifted to the left toward a dressing mirror. In the reflection she saw Aspen Harper behind her, and she did in fact have a small-caliber gun pressed against her ribs.

"You're the reason for all of my problems," she continued. "Jane will never want anyone else as long as you're around."

Ari didn't understand. "What are you talking about? Jane is my friend. We're not romantically involved."

Fingers pried into her elbow and her body whirled around. Her gaze immediately fell to the gun now pressed into her chest, but when she looked up, she realized she was not looking at Aspen Harper—but rather Courtney Belmont in a wig.

Courtney smiled knowingly. "You just don't see it, and neither does she. But if you were gone, she would. She'd be lost without you, and she'd finally reveal her true self to someone else. She'd stop being the slutty tramp that sleeps with everyone."

"You do know I have a girlfriend."

Courtney shook her head. "It'll never last, Ari. I've watched you with Molly. That woman is so uptight. She'll never love you the way Jane does."

216

She stared at her but said nothing, knowing she could never change Courtney's mind.

"Now, this is what we're gonna do," Courtney said, pulling her toward the exit. "I know there's a back door out of here. We're leaving together, but unfortunately you'll disappear—forever."

Ari quickly assessed the situation. If she angered Courtney, she could be shot, but she didn't have any other options. No one knew she was here, and the party was in full swing. It could be a long while before anyone noticed she was missing. "Why are you so sure killing me will change things with Jane?" she asked meekly.

The gun poked her roughly in the gut and she winced in pain. "Shut up!" Courtney barked. "Now walk, and don't say another word."

Ari took a few steps slowly toward a door behind the manager's chair. It was the private exit, and she knew that it led out to the back alley. No doubt the Dodge Viper was already parked nearby. Ari knew if she got in that car, Molly or Biz would probably never find her. A few more steps and she passed the open door of the manager's restroom, her intended destination. Again the bizarre picture of Courtney holding her hostage appeared momentarily in the bathroom mirror—as well as Molly's face. She automatically stopped, and Courtney was caught off-balance. In that instant, Molly lunged and Ari pulled away from Courtney's grasp. A gunshot rang out as Molly and Courtney crashed into the coffee table. The gun skittered across the floor, and to her horror, Molly's face smashed against the hearth of the nearby fireplace, knocking her unconscious. Ari screamed and ran toward the gun, but Courtney was closer. Her fingers wrapped around the grip, and she fired. Ari jumped out of the bullet's path and scrambled for the door that led back to the party. The discharge of another bullet told her that the deranged woman was following her. She sailed through the back room as another bullet ripped past her and shattered the glass dividing the back room from the main dance floor.

"Gun!" she screamed.

Partygoers scattered off the dance floor, headed for the exits and the dark corners of the bar. She hurled herself over the DJ's booth just as the gun blasted a hole through the cutout of Marilyn Monroe. When Ari stuck her head out, Courtney fired, but only a harsh click sounded from the gun. She was out of bullets. She dropped it and immediately charged for the motorcycle parked in the corner. She hopped on and the engine roared to life. Ari watched the bike careen toward her, and just as she thought she might be killed by her father's birthday present, Biz lunged from the side and smashed Courtney in the face with a waitress's tray. The force sent her backward and she lost control of the bike. Both machine and rider skidded into a picture display of Ari.

Biz ran to Ari. "Are you all right?"

"I'm fine. I've got to check on Molly. She's hurt."

Biz pointed to the back room. "No, here she comes."

Molly staggered over, holding her head. She reached for Ari and pulled her close. "I thought I was going to lose you."

Andre ran up to them. "Mol, are you okay?"

"Where the hell were you?"

He sighed deeply. "In the bathroom. Sorry," he added.

Molly nodded her forgiveness, and they moved her to a chair. Ari's friends slowly reemerged from the bowels of the bar, and the noise level increased as they began to exchange versions of the event. Above the voices came a bloodcurdling scream. Everyone turned to see Jane sitting on top of Courtney, throttling her. Biz stood over Jane, trying to suppress a laugh.

"I'm going to kill you, you bitch!"

Despite Jane's fingers wrapped around her neck, Courtney tried to explain. "Jane, I love you. We're meant to be together. Ari's not right for you."

"What the hell is she talking about?" Molly asked.

Ari sighed. "It's complicated. Guys never have these problems."

"You drugged me!" Jane raged.

Andre walked to Jane and grabbed her shoulders. "C'mon, Jane. Get off her."

Jane started to release Courtney and then changed her mind. "You ruined Ari's party!" she yelled as she clamped her hands back on Courtney's throat and smashed the woman's head against the tile floor.

Locked in an embrace, Ari and Molly watched from a distance. Brian leaned over and said to his sister, "Don't you think you and Andre should do something, seeing as you are cops? Your fellow brethren will be showing up any moment now, and I'd hate to see Jane be arrested."

Molly shrugged and kissed Ari on the forehead. "I don't see anything. I'm still in shock from my concussion."

Brian laughed a little and then looked at his sister seriously.

"Oh, all right," Molly said.

She broke free of Ari, and with Andre and Biz's help, she pried the women apart. The uniformed cops arrived and put Courtney in handcuffs while Ari sat at a table waiting for Molly to finish giving her statement to the detective in charge. Jane dropped into a chair next to her best friend and took her hand.

"I'm sorry your party was a bust."

She patted Jane's arm. "Honey, this was a great party, and except for that one little part where Courtney was shooting at me, I had a wonderful time."

Jane chuckled and kissed her on the cheek. "You are the most important person in my life. You know that, right?"

Ari smiled, remembering Courtney's words. She couldn't believe Jane was madly attracted to her, but she knew she loved her in a way that no one else ever would. "I know, sweetie."

Both Teri and Biz joined them, and Teri pulled her chair behind Jane and began massaging her shoulders. "I can't believe she was the stalker. If I'd known that she was using those beautiful flowers to hurt you, I would have shot her with my nail gun."

Jane patted her leg and leaned against her. Soon they were laughing and cuddling. *If only it could work between them,* Ari thought.

She looked at Biz, who was staring at her. "Thanks for helping me."

Biz shook her head in disagreement. "I don't accept your thanks. This was my fault. I didn't do my job very well. The cops are saying that the Dodge Viper out back is Aspen's. I should have followed up on that connection sooner. I'll bet she was blackmailing Aspen over what happened in Albuquerque."

Ari shrugged. "Maybe. But no one could have known that Courtney would fall for Jane. I'm just glad you and Molly were here."

"Me and Molly," Biz repeated. "We're quite a pair." Awkwardness passed between them and Biz looked over at the motorcycle. Brian had righted the bike, and it sat in the corner waiting for Ari. "Do you know how to ride?"

She laughed. "Of course not. That's why my father's gift is entirely appropriate."

Biz shook her head. "Come again?"

"Never mind. It would take too long to explain."

"Sounds like a story there. I told you my story, so maybe someday you'll tell me yours."

She glanced at Biz's incredible brown eyes, the gold flecks shining. "Maybe someday."

Biz stood to leave and glanced at the motorcycle. "And if you ever want to learn to ride this thing, call me."

"I'm not sure I'll even keep it."

"I think you should. There is nothing sexier than a beautiful woman straddling a motorcycle."

She could feel her cheeks coloring again. Biz certainly had a power over her. "I thought we agreed you wouldn't flirt anymore?"

"We did, but I couldn't help it."

Biz stuck her hands in her pockets and headed for the door. Before she left, she turned back and gazed at her with an odd expression. It gave her the feeling she was missing out on something. An opportunity was passing that she might regret. She glanced over at Molly, who was giving orders to several uniformed officers. Hideaway had become a crime scene, and Molly was in full cop mode. When she looked back at the exit, Biz was gone.

Chapter Thirty-eight
Saturday, October 21st
3:15 AM

The ride back to Molly's apartment was quiet. Ari and Molly snuggled together in the back of Lynne's Prius while soft jazz filled the interior. Molly had refused to go to the ER after one of the paramedics had checked her out and determined her concussion was minor. Vicky had slipped her a painkiller as they departed, and she was clearly starting to feel its effects. As she shifted in her seat, a soft moan escaped her lips.

"How much does it hurt?" Ari asked.

"I'm okay," she answered, and Ari knew she was lying. The only girl in a family of boys, Molly learned early that to admit pain gained her the immediate title of wussy. Her fall against the stone hearth had nearly broken the bones in her face, and an enormous purple bruise was forming around her right temple. Molly pulled her closer and kissed the top of her head. "I'm sorry about your birthday," she whispered.

Ari stroked her thigh, realizing that her words to Jane were true. Up until the confrontation with Courtney, she had enjoyed her party immensely, mainly because of Molly's presence—Molly's love. The thought created a shroud of comfort around her, and she suddenly felt secure in their relationship. She no longer worried about when Molly would declare her love. She realized it was all around her.

After reassuring Lynne and Brian several times that they did not need babysitters, the straight couple went home, and they quickly disappeared into the bathroom for a shower. Streaming jets washed away the adrenalin and emotions until only fatigue remained, and when they slipped into bed, the only intention was sleep.

"I think we'll really have to celebrate your birthday in the morning," Molly mumbled.

Ari lightly touched Molly's lips with her own. "That's fine, darling. It can wait."

Molly kissed her again, and again, until a flicker of passion ignited. She rolled on top of her, their breasts pressed together. Ari spread her legs, an invitation Molly willingly accepted.

"Are you sure you're up for this?" Ari asked.

Molly grinned wickedly and her long fingers answered Ari's question. Their lovemaking was a momentary flame that burned only for a short time and left them spent in each other's arms.

"I want to give you your gift now," Molly said suddenly. She reached into her nightstand and withdrew a slender box wrapped perfectly in gold paper. "Obviously I didn't do the wrap job."

Ari carefully pulled apart the end of the paper, eliciting a chuckle from Molly. She shook her head, well aware that Molly believed unwrapping gifts was more of a "seek and destroy" mission.

She gazed at the gold necklace and her eyes filled with tears. "It's beautiful, baby. Will you help me put it on?"

Molly undid the clasp and fastened the chain around her

223

neck. She went to the dresser mirror and admired the gold rope, a smile on her face. *Yes, the proof of Molly's love is all around me.*

Molly appeared behind her and kissed her neck. "Don't tell me you're up for more," Ari joked.

"No, but I love you."

Her jaw dropped. Molly's delivery was so casual, sounding as if she made the statement every day.

She turned to Molly, caressing her unharmed cheek, probing her gaze for regret or remorse. She saw only earnest longing, and she thought that Molly had wanted to say the words as much as she had wanted to hear them. Still somewhat cautious of overwhelming her, she replied simply, "Baby, I love you, too."

A kiss sealed the moment, and they returned to bed, unable to stand any longer. Lying in Molly's arms, she fell into a dreamy state. She and Molly were standing on a cliff, the swirling sea beneath them. Then Molly took her hand, and they stepped away from the precipice and strolled toward a sunny garden path.

In a matter of minutes, Ari was dozing against Molly, who remained in a haze, her brain unwilling to entirely shut off, and the effects of the painkiller forcing her body into a relaxed state that conflicted with her racing mind. She snuggled with Ari for three hours, until the painkiller wore off and freed her mind to enjoy all of its anxiety and fear.

She stole into the living room and settled on the couch with a glass of Scotch. She sipped it slowly, savoring the descent of the liquid down her throat, which seemed to tighten with each thought of their encounter just a few short hours ago. All of the pieces in her mind were fragments, the moments that totaled up to three words, the ones she'd avoided for most of her adult life. She closed her eyes and realized she'd said it first.

For a split second the future had been clear to her, full of loss and abandonment that sunk Molly's heart into a deep hole. As Ari's naked body had stood in front of the mirror, turned away, she imagined her walking out the door—and into Biz's waiting arms—leaving with someone who truly appreciated her and saw her incredible gifts. And had Courtney's aim been better, she would have lost Ari forever tonight. She saw her empty life without Ari, and she had momentarily lost her breath.

She had declared her love for Ari knowing that she was waiting, wanting to hear those words on her birthday more than she could have ever wanted any material object that Molly could have afforded. She had given her the most coveted of presents, and now she worried it would be at the ultimate cost. She drained the glass and shoved it away from herself, nearly propelling it off the coffee table. She lowered her head and took deep breaths, willing the panic attack to pass before Ari awoke.

Chapter Thirty-nine
Saturday, October 21st
9:48 AM

When Molly's eyes fluttered open, the first thing she saw was Ari's long legs extended across the stools of her breakfast bar. She wore only a police T-shirt over her panties, and Molly was instantly aroused. She sat up and Ari turned around, smiling. Her long hair flowed around her face, and she looked absolutely beautiful.

"Hey there, sleepy."

"Hi. When did you get up?"

"About a half hour ago." Ari slid off the stool and went to the kitchen. She brought Molly a steaming mug of coffee and joined her on the couch, draping her incredible legs over Molly's hips. They stared at each other, Ari fingering the gold rope around her neck. "I love this."

She nodded. "I can tell."

"How's your face?"

She touched the enormous bruise and flinched. "Still hurts."

Ari set her mug down and took her hand. "I love you."

"I love you," she replied automatically. Ari stared at her, and she instantly felt uncomfortable. "Is everything okay?"

"You can take it back if you need to."

She swallowed hard. *How did she know?*

As if she could read her mind, Ari said, "I found the Scotch glass in the sink. At first I thought you'd come out here because your face was hurting, but then I saw the glass, and I knew."

Molly's gaze dropped to the floor. "I don't know what to say." She glanced at Ari, and all she saw was concern. "I can't explain."

"Just tell me how you feel. Do you care for me?"

She squeezed her hand and stared at her. "I've never felt this way about anyone." She opened her mouth but words failed her. *How could she explain?* "It's overwhelming," she said finally. "I do love you, and I don't want to take it back. I'm glad we both said it, but I'm scared, and worried and paranoid. Too many emotions and I can't see clearly, I guess." She paused, afraid of what Ari was thinking. "So, what do we do now?"

Ari looked up and laughed. "Have breakfast?"

She smiled and felt the knot around her heart loosen—a little. "I think I just need more time to get used to it."

Ari kissed her. "I know. And you've given me enough for now."

They retreated to the kitchen and found the ingredients for omelets. Once the eggs were cooking, Ari wandered to the piano and shuffled through the pages of Itchy's open file. Molly had brought it home earlier in the week, hoping she could find clues—clues they didn't need anymore.

"What's this?" Ari asked.

She realized Ari was holding a copy of the mysterious scrap of paper with the words *Here to Help!* printed at the bottom and the numbers on the other side. "We never figured that out. Itchy had it in his backpack. We thought it was an important lead that would help us catch his killer, but we didn't need it. I'm wondering if it had something to do with the leak, but I don't think we'll ever figure it out. All the brass will care about is that John Rondo's dead and so is his accomplice. Case closed."

"Interesting," Ari said.

Molly dropped the bread into the toaster and glanced up. "Why?"

"I'm just wondering why a street person would have an original piece of stationery from a title company."

Molly froze. "That's from a title company?"

"Uh-huh. American National."

Molly's eyes narrowed. "Are you sure?"

"I'm positive. I've got lots of their stuff in my files unfortunately. Jane and I hate dealing with them because their slogan is worthless. They are the *least* helpful and ethical company in the valley. We never let our clients use them if we can help it."

Ari paused, as if waiting for Molly to say something, but she was too surprised, and all of the switches in her brain were clicking. Perhaps this was still important. Perhaps it would lead to the mole. "So if the numbers were written on stationery from a title company—"

"Then I'll bet that the numbers are part of an address." Ari held out the scrap of paper. "Why would a street person need an address?"

He wouldn't, but the mole would.

Publications from
BELLA BOOKS, INC.
The best in contemporary lesbian fiction
P.O. Box 10543, Tallahassee, FL 32302
Phone: 800-729-4992
www.bellabooks.com

WITHOUT WARNING: Book one in the Shaken series by KG MacGregor. *Without Warning* is the story of their courageous journey through adversity, and their promise of steadfast love. 978-1-59493-120-8 $13.95

THE CANDIDATE by Tracey Richardson. Presidential candidate Jane Kincaid had always expected the road to the White House would exact a high personal toll. She just never knew how high until forced to choose between her heart and her political destiny. 978-1-59493-133-8 $13.95

TALL IN THE SADDLE by Karin Kallmaker, Barbara Johnson, Therese Szymanski and Julia Watts. The playful quartet that penned the acclaimed *Once Upon A Dyke* and *Stake Through the Heart* are back and now turning to the Wild (and Very Hot) West to bring you another collection of erotically charged, action-packed, tales. 978-1-59493-106-2 $15.95

IN THE NAME OF THE FATHER by Gerri Hill. In this highly anticipated sequel to *Hunter's Way*, Dallas homicide detectives Tori Hunter and Samantha Kennedy investigate the murder of a Catholic priest who is found naked and strangled to death. 978-1-59493-108-6 $13.95

IT'S ALL SMOKE AND MIRRORS: The First Chronicles of Shawn Donnelly by Therese Szymanski. Join Therese Szymanski as she takes a walk on the sillier side of the gritty crime-scene detective novel and introduces readers to her newest alternate personality—Shawn Donnelly. 978-1-59493-117-8 $13.95

THE ROAD HOME by Frankie J. Jones. As Lynn finds herself in one adventure after another, she discovers that true wealth may have very little to do with money after all. 978-1-59493-110-9 $13.95

IN DEEP WATERS: CRUISING THE SEAS by Karin Kallmaker and Radclyffe. Book passage on a deliciously sensual Mediterranean cruise with tour guides Radclyffe and Karin Kallmaker. 978-1-59493-111-6 $15.95

ALL THAT GLITTERS by Peggy J. Herring. Life is good for retired Army colonel Marcel Robicheaux. Marcel is unprepared for the turn her life will take. She soon finds herself in the pursuit of a lifetime—searching for her missing mother and lover. 978-1-59493-107-9 $13.95

OUT OF LOVE by KG MacGregor. For Carmen Delallo and Judith O'Shea, falling in love proves to be the easy part. 978-1-59493-105-5 $13.95

BORDERLINE by Terri Breneman. Assistant prosecuting attorney Toni Barston returns in the sequel to *Anticipation*. 978-1-59493-99-7 $13.95

PAST REMEMBERING by Lyn Denison. What would it take to melt Peri's cool exterior? Any involvement on Asha's part would be simply asking for trouble and heartache . . . wouldn't it? 978-1-59493-103-1 $13.95

ASPEN'S EMBERS by Diane Tremain Braund. Will Aspen choose the woman she loves. . . or the forest she hopes to preserve. 978-1-59493-102-4 $14.95

THE COTTAGE by Gerri Hill. *The Cottage* is the heartbreaking story of two women who meet by chance . . . or did they? A love so destined it couldn't be denied . . . stolen moments to be cherished forever. 978-1-59493-096-6 $13.95

FANTASY: Untrue Stories of Lesbian Passion edited by Barbara Johnson and Therese Szymanski. Lie back and let Bella's bad girls take you on an erotic journey through the greatest bedtime stories never told. 978-1-59493-101-7 $15.95

SISTERS' FLIGHT by Jeanne G'Fellers. *Sisters' Flight* is the highly anticipated sequel to *No Sister of Mine* and *Sister Lost, Sister Found.* 978-1-59493-116-1 $13.95

BRAGGIN' RIGHTS by Kenna White. Taylor Fleming is a thirty-six-year-old Texas rancher who covets her independence. She finds her cowgirl independence tested by neighboring rancher Jen Holland. 978-1-59493-095-9 $13.95

BRILLIANT by Ann Roberts. Respected sociology professor, Diane Cole finds her views on love challenged by her own heart, as she fights the attraction she feels for a woman half her age. 978-1-59493-115-4 $13.95

THE EDUCATION OF ELLIE by Jackie Calhoun. When Ellie sees her childhood friend for the first time in thirty years she is tempted to resume their long lost friendship. But with the years come a lot of baggage and the two women struggle with who they are now while fighting the painful memories of their first parting. Will they be able to move past their history to start again? 978-1-59493-092-8 $13.95

DATE NIGHT CLUB by Saxon Bennett. *Date Night Club* is a dark romantic comedy about the pitfalls of dating in your thirties . . . 978-1-59493-094-2 $13.95

PLEASE FORGIVE ME by Megan Carter. Laurel Becker is on the verge of losing the two most important things in her life—her current lover, Elaine Alexander, and the Lavender Page bookstore. Will Elaine and Laurel manage to work through their misunderstandings and rebuild their life together? 978-1-59493-091-1 $13.95

WHISKEY AND OAK LEAVES by Jaime Clevenger. Meg meets June, a single woman running a horse ranch in the California Sierra foothills. The two become quick friends and it isn't long before Meg is looking for more than just a friendship. But June has no interest in developing a deeper relationship with Meg. She is, after all, not the least bit interested in women . . . or is she? Neither of these two women is prepared for what lies ahead . . . 978-1-59493-093-5 $13.95

SUMTER POINT by KG MacGregor. As Audie surrenders her heart to Beth, she begins to distance herself from the reckless habits of her youth. Just as they're ready to meet in the middle, their future is thrown into doubt by a duty Beth can't ignore. It all comes to a head on the river at Sumter Point. 978-1-59493-089-8 $13.95

THE TARGET by Gerri Hill. Sara Michaels is the daughter of a prominent senator who has been receiving death threats against his family. In an effort to protect Sara, the FBI recruits homicide detective Jaime Hutchinson to secretly provide the protection they are so certain Sara will need. Will Sara finally figure out who is behind the death threats? And will Jaime realize the truth—and be able to save Sara before it's too late? 978-1-59493-082-9 $13.95